Talk Teeny

Talk Teeny

A NOVEL TOLD IN VIGNETTES

CHERYL FAIR

ENTITY PRESS

Acknowledgments

First, to my husband, George Hagegeorge for his patience, humor, and unwavering support throughout this work. I am also grateful to: (in alphabetical order) Rosie Behr, Otis A. Brown Jr., Michael Brown, Jennifer Keith Ciattei, Marjorie Collins, Tom Culotta, Sharron Dinkins, Tom DiVenti, Alvin Fair, Frank Fair, June Beauchamp Fair, Debi Gonzales, Clynthia Burton Graham, Josephine Ma, Paula Millet, Justin Petrone, Rebecca Quintana, Kim Talboo.

CONTENTS

PART ONE

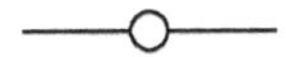

0   Prelude

Late afternoon light cuts through the glass block window in slanted bars across the wide-plank floor. The room smells faintly of beer, smoke, and something fried hours ago. It's southeastern Virginia, 1953. Fats Domino plays on the jukebox.

Behind the bar, a woman takes inventory, counting bottles, making small pencil marks on a pad. A brunette with porcelain skin, wearing a mid-calf pencil skirt, sits on a barstool smoking. In front of her is a Coke in a glass, a paper straw leaning against the rim. Beside her, perched on another stool like a doll set carefully on a shelf, is a tiny girl in a crisply ironed dress.

The child faces the room, not the bar. One arm remains extended, her fingers resting against her mother's hip—not holding, just touching. Her eyes move deliberately, pausing on her father, on the men around him, then back again.

Her father Hugh is the one with hair like Superman's and pale gray-blue eyes. His khaki work shirt is rolled high enough to show a bird-in-flight tattoo on his bicep. He laughs louder than the others.

Five men stand around a tall table, bottles of beer in their hands, debating whether to start a craps game in the alley.

The girl is not quite two. She's small for her age, very pale, dark-haired, with a steady, unblinking stare that makes strangers hesitate. A man who has been drinking drifts over, bends slightly at the waist, and says,

"Talk, Teeny."

The bartender and the girl's mother exchange a look—a smirk, a wink. The mother swivels her stool just enough to keep the man in view. The child looks at him long enough to decide something, then meets his eyes.

"What do you want me to say?" Her voice is unmistakably a child's, but the phrasing isn't. The man straightens, startled. The bartender laughs.

"See? I told ya."

One person drifts closer. Then another. The child notices the shift before anyone speaks. Her mother nudges her gently.

"Tell him about the cigarettes."

The child turns only after the nudge. She points toward the display on the wall carefully, one pack at a time, not rushing, not skipping, her finger landing squarely before each name.

"Chesterfield. Lucky Strike. L & M. Camels. Pall Mall. Viceroy. Old Gold. Philip Morris. Winston. Kents. That's what Mommy smokes." Her mother takes a drag. Coins appear on the bar. The child watches where they land before looking back at her mother. Everyone laughs.

It's the hour when the shipyard men begin filing in. Hard hats under arms, lunch pails swinging. Their skin is dark and glossy from the sun. The bartender starts opening beers in advance, lining them up. At first glance they all look the same—dirty, tired, ready to loosen up. But one of them moves differently. Leroy has the same tattooed arms and pale eyes as Hugh, but his face is softer, more inward. Wire rimmed glasses sit slightly crooked on his nose.

Leroy takes his beer, nods to the bartender, and walks toward the table where his brother is holding court.

Hugh breaks off mid-sentence.

"What the hell took you so long?"

"Missed you at work today," Leroy says, squinting slightly. After a few minutes the men head out the back door toward the alley.

Not long after, a woman comes in alone. She waves toward the bar.

"Hey, Ellie." Then, glancing at the child, "What're you up to, Teeny?" Eleanor pats the empty stool beside her.

"Saved you a seat, Doris. Pretty dress."

Doris sits. She's Eleanor's age but looks older—too thin, her face worn, something fragile in the way she moves that makes people want to take care around her. She scans the room.

"Has Leroy been by yet?"

"In the alley," Eleanor says.

Teeny talks steadily, naming what she sees, reporting what has already happened. When no one responds, she keeps going anyway. The women decide on crab cakes when the bartender has a minute. Tennessee Ernie Ford is loud now, singing "Catfish Boogie."

By the time the plates are cleared, Teeny shifts her weight. The room has changed. She wants down.

Hugh and Leroy come back in through the rear, having left the game unfinished. Doris leans forward and gives Leroy a quick kiss.

"I ordered you one to go. Let's get you home. Fed. Cleaned up."

Eleanor lifts Teeny onto her hip and asks Hugh how he did. He gives her a lopsided grin.

"I reckon I did alright."

Teeny squirms, talks, twists. Hugh laughs.

"That kid was vaccinated with a phonograph needle." He pays the tab. Eleanor leaves an extra dollar tucked beneath her plate.

Outside, the air smells of salt. Seagulls cry overhead. Teeny is passed from arm to arm as they walk. She doesn't protest. She watches.

They stop in front of a big brown clapboard house with a wrap-around porch. Hugh and Eleanor go in the first door, just past the vestibule. Doris and Leroy head upstairs.

"See you tomorrow," they call over their shoulders.

Eleanor puts the little girl to bed. Together they say the words:

> *Now I lay me down to sleep.*
> *I pray the Lord my soul to keep.*
> *If I should die before I wake,*
> *I pray the Lord my soul to take.*

Eleanor switches on the nightlight and closes the door.

Hugh, mostly sober but drunk all day today, wrestles his shirt over his arms and drops it with his belt on the chair. He lies down on the rug in front of the fireplace. No fire. Just the andirons and the screen on the marble hearth.

By the time Eleanor comes out, he's asleep. She stands at his feet for a moment, sighs, then bends to pull off his boots. He grumbles but doesn't wake. She hesitates, then covers him with a blanket.

She makes herself a cup of tea, brings it into the living room, and turns on the television.

DUN DA DUN DUNNNNNN.

She looks up as the announcer says, "Ladies and gentlemen, the story you are about to see is true. The names have been changed to protect the innocent."

Hugh snores. The television keeps talking.

1   Cards

Even early in the morning, the heat has already settled in. The windows
are open and the fans hum steadily, pushing warm air from one room to
the next without really cooling anything down. Teeny is sunk deep into
the big stuffed chair in the living room, her small body nearly swallowed
by the cushions, her eyes fixed on the television.

Eleanor has just finished in the kitchen—Hugh sent off to work,
dishes rinsed and stacked—and now she claims the couch with a cup of
tea. She takes a few careful sips, then sets the cup down and reaches for a
magazine from the end table. She leans back, crosses her legs, and lets one
shoe dangle loose from her toe.

She has barely started an article about Tony Curtis playing Harry
Houdini when a soft cough sounds from the hallway, followed by a polite
tap at the apartment door. Eleanor places the magazine on the coffee table,
next to a deck of playing cards, and calls out, without looking at Teeny,

"It's Aunt Doris."

Teeny doesn't respond. She's laughing at the television.

"Mornin', Ellie!" Doris says brightly when the door opens. "Are you
ready to read my cards?"

They decide on the kitchen. Eleanor scoops up the deck from the
coffee table, and the two women move toward the yellow Formica dinette.
Teeny stays where she is, mesmerized by a commercial, repeating the lines
back in a sing-song voice.

"When they have a headache, Alka-Seltzer brings relief!"

From the kitchen, Eleanor keeps one eye on her daughter as she
shuffles. The cards slip smoothly through her hands, flipped and gathered
with an ease that looks practiced but not showy.

"I always wondered," Doris says, watching, "how you learned to
read fortunes."

"My mother read cards," Eleanor says, not pausing.

"Do you ever read your own?"

"Sometimes." Eleanor sets the deck down squarely in front of Doris.
"Cut it into three even piles—left to right—with your left hand.
And think about your question."

Doris's hand trembles slightly as she does it. Eleanor reassembles the piles, pressing them together into a single deck, face down in her palm.

Teeny toddles in.

"Hi Aunt Doris! I'm Speedy Alka-Seltzer!"

Doris laughs and pats the top of her head.

"Yes, you are."

Teeny cranes forward, trying to climb up and see the cards, but Eleanor gives her the look. The girl pauses, then redirects herself to her small wooden table and chairs—Hugh's handiwork, made from scrap lumber. She pours pretend tea from her toy set, serving a stuffed rabbit and a plastic chicken seated side by side.

Eleanor lays the cards out face up in a careful, complicated pattern.

"A journey across water," she says, "within three."

"Three what?" Doris asks.

"Days. Weeks. Months. Years." Eleanor's voice stays even. She continues. "There's illness to watch for. And love—and sadness—from a man with brown hair and light eyes."

They nod together.

"Leroy," Doris says.

After a pause, Doris asks,

"And my wish?"

Eleanor draws three more cards. Her mouth tightens almost imperceptibly.

"It's not going to happen," she says, "not in the foreseeable future." She looks up and meets Doris's eyes. "I'm sorry."

Eleanor knows the wish. It's always the same one.

A sudden clatter breaks the moment. Teeny is standing on top of her little table, reaching toward the parakeet cage with a toy teacup held high.

Eleanor is on her feet instantly, lifting the girl down.

"You know Daddy's parakeet doesn't drink tea."

They laugh as Teeny is set back into her chair. Just then the white angora cat winds around Eleanor's legs, wearing a doll's dress and meowing plaintively.

"When did you dress the kitty?" Eleanor asks.

"She's my baby!" Teeny says, delighted.

Doris smiles, then asks,

"Are you meeting Hugh at the job site today?"

Eleanor reaches for the box of graham crackers and hands one to Teeny.

"It's Friday. You know I am. If I don't remind him about the bills, he'll spend the whole paycheck when he cashes it at the bar."

"We'll see you this evening," Doris says.

The fans keep humming. The cards stay where they are on the table.

2   Friday

Eleanor crosses the construction site with Teeny balanced on her hip, stepping through the dried mud ruts as if they've been set there for her alone. The ground is cracked and uneven, but she moves easily, careful without looking careful, each step already decided. She has done this before.

Hugh is a short distance ahead, driving nails into place. He is shirtless, his khaki carpenter's hat pulled low to shade his eyes. The rhythm of his hammer is steady and unbroken. The other men keep working, glancing up as she passes, aware but silent. She feels their eyes and knows what they see: that she belongs here, that she belongs to Hugh.

He finishes the last few nails just as they reach him. Without looking up, he says,

"I'm about ready to knock off. Let me get my shirt on."

He pulls a khaki shirt from a stack of lumber, still clean in the late sun. As he slips it on, Eleanor notices the corner of his paycheck envelope sticking out of the pocket. Another small certainty. Another step already taken.

"Foreman came by at lunch," Hugh says. "Dropped the checks. Let's cash this and get something to eat."

Teeny talks the whole time, naming everything she can see. Her words float around them, filling the air without changing its direction. Eleanor shifts her daughter higher on her hip.

"You're getting to be a big girl," she says, and feels the weight of the moment settle—not happiness exactly, but the quiet solidity of routine.

They walk to the bar nearest the job site as the men begin putting their tools away, the workweek folding itself up. The sun hangs low and heavy. Friday takes its place, as predictable as a reading laid out on a table: the paycheck, the drinks, the walk home.

Later, they leave the bar together. Neon glows against the asphalt. Hugh walks carefully now, each step deliberate, as if he can will himself sober through attention alone. Eleanor carries Teeny the entire way, her grip steady, her arm beginning to ache.

Something is off, but she does not name it.

Inside the apartment, Hugh stops short. The bird cage sits open. The parakeet is gone. Nearby, the white angora cat crouches with blue feathers stuck to its face.

The change in Hugh is instant. His face hardens, and what follows happens too quickly to interrupt. The cat hisses and scrambles, but Hugh keeps at it until it disappears under the couch. The violence is sudden and absolute, a sharp tear in the fabric of the evening.

Teeny screams. Eleanor takes her into the other room, rocking her, murmuring comfort that doesn't quite reach either of them. The sounds behind her fade. Hugh stumbles out into the night, leaving the apartment vibrating with what has just happened.

Eleanor dresses Teeny in flannel pajamas and lies down beside her for just a minute. The room darkens. Sleep presses in, heavy and insistent. Hours pass.

She wakes to the rattle of the door in the hallway. Quietly, she closes the bedroom door and slips into the living room, lighting a cigarette. Hugh stands there in the dim light, sober now or close enough, holding a box and something small and red.

"What've you got?" she asks.

"Sonofabitch won't kill any more birds now," he says.

She recognizes the red object—an ether capsule from the job site. He pulls the cat from its hiding place, leaving a dark trail behind it. He disappears into the backyard.

Eleanor knows what will happen. It'll lose consciousness quickly. It won't suffer any longer. Relief rises in her, unwanted but undeniable.

In a few hours, they will pack the car and leave again. This apartment will close behind them; another place folded into memory. The chain of events feels unbroken—set in motion long before the hammer stopped, before the paycheck was cashed, before she crossed the construction site with a child on her hip, following steps that always seem to lead to the same place.

3 The Big Chair

Teeny thought of the big overstuffed chair in the new living room as hers.
She had claimed it early.

Barely two years old—small even for her age—her body nearly
disappeared into the deep cushions. When she climbed up, the chair held
her the way arms might have, swallowing her legs, cradling her back.
From there she could watch television or simply sit and exist. It made her
feel safe.

One afternoon, Hugh's old friend Caleb came by the apartment
looking for him. Hugh wasn't home yet, but Eleanor invited Caleb in
and told him to make himself comfortable. She went into the kitchen to
make coffee.

Caleb sat down in the big chair.

Teeny didn't know him. She knew her mother, though, and Eleanor
didn't seem alarmed, so Teeny stayed where she was, watching. But the
longer the man sat there—his long legs stretched out, his weight sinking
into the cushions—the more wrong it felt. This stranger had taken her
place. And Eleanor had let him.

Teeny toddled around the chair, circling him slowly, her eyes fixed
on his face. He didn't notice her at first. When she began tugging on
his pant leg, he startled, clearly unsure what to do with a baby at his feet.
He called out to Eleanor, a little too loudly,

"I think she wants to sit in my lap."

Before anyone could object, he lifted Teeny up and set her on his
knee. He smiled at her uncertainly, trying to talk the way adults do when
they've been told a child is special. A talker. He asked her questions. He
made faces. He didn't realize she wasn't amused.

Teeny waited.

Then she placed her small hands on either side of his face and turned
it toward her. The closeness made him laugh, nervous and surprised. She
looked him straight in the eyes.

"Get out of my chair, you big nasty jerk!"

The room went very still.

Caleb's mouth fell open.

"Did she just say what I think she said?" he asked Eleanor, half laughing, half stunned.

Eleanor laughed too, untroubled.

"Yes," she said. "She wants to sit in the chair by herself."

Later, after Hugh came home and Caleb had gone, Eleanor told him what had happened. They laughed about it together, replaying the words, the audacity of them.

Teeny was already back in her chair, folded into the cushions, restored to her proper place.

4   Scar

Teeny had walked early. Eight months. By two, she moved through rooms with confidence, a small body already certain it belonged wherever it went.

That afternoon Eleanor sat on the sofa with a book open in her lap. A glass bottle of Coke rested on the end table beside her. Teeny played on the rug, then noticed the bottle. She wanted it. She crossed the room without asking.

Eleanor felt the movement more than she saw it. When she looked up, Teeny had the bottle in both hands. Eleanor reached for her at once, already picturing the glass, the weight, the way a child didn't know how to be careful yet.

Teeny laughed and ran.

Eleanor stood too fast. Teeny's foot caught the edge of the marble hearth. The bottle shattered as it hit her mouth.

There was blood everywhere—bright, sudden. Eleanor screamed and scooped the child up, Coke and glass and fear all over her hands. She ran to the doctor's office a block away, not stopping to think, only knowing the baby was hurt.

The doctor lived above his office. His wife answered the door, already pulling them inside. Teeny was carried into the exam room while the doctor came down the stairs, pulling on his coat, his breath thick with alcohol.

Eleanor noticed. She had no choice.

The doctor said stitches were necessary and set to work. Eleanor held Teeny still, whispering, fighting her own tears. The child's lip swelled and bled, her face slack with shock. Eleanor looked away when she could.

When it started to heal, it looked wrong.

The scar looked thick and uneven, cutting into the line of Teeny's upper lip. Eleanor stared at it, said aloud what she believed.

"This is going to ruin her looks." "She'll be scarred for life."

When Eleanor brought Teeny back to have the stitches removed, the doctor's wife saw the child and said quietly, not quite to herself,

"He really botched that."

Over time, the mark faded. It thinned into a pale line, barely visible unless you knew where to look. Most people never noticed it at all.

Eleanor always did. To her, it was everything.

5   Shoes and Skates

There were doctors for everything.

Teeny had started walking very early, but her ankles tipped inward. Eleanor noticed. One of Teeny's doctors was just for her feet. Her shoes had to be special and were ordered from somewhere else. Eleanor said they were expensive.

First there were white high-topped baby shoes. Then shoes for a little girl. There were only two kinds: brown oxfords or dark red Mary Janes. Even when Teeny was two, Eleanor held them up, side by side and asked,

"Which ones?"

Teeny always chose the Mary Janes.

The shoes were heavy. The heels were a little higher on the one side than the other. Inside them was something hard that kept her feet from turning in. They looked like normal shoes, just stiff and serious. The foot doctor said they would fix her walking and that her feet would grow the right way. Eleanor listened carefully and did what the doctor said.

Most days Teeny wore the red shoes. On Sundays she wore different ones. They were black patent leather with a thin strap across the top. They shone. Teeny loved them. She wished she could wear them every day. She wished there were more than two choices.

Before she was three, Teeny asked for roller skates. Eleanor asked the foot doctor if that was allowed. He said yes.

Hugh and Eleanor clamped the heavy metal skates over the red Mary Janes. They tightened them until they didn't wiggle. Teeny stayed very still while they worked. When they were done, she felt taller.

She wore the skate key on a ribbon around her neck. It bumped against her chest when she moved. She could go as fast as she wanted.

There were no other children to skate with. That didn't matter. Teeny liked the sound the wheels made and the feeling of speed. She liked the way the world slid past her, quick and bright, while she stayed upright and moving.

6   Art

One of the apartments Eleanor and Hugh lived in sat directly across the street from Buckroe Beach. It was a first-floor place with a wide front porch, like nearly every house on that block. The porch dipped slightly in the middle and smelled like salt and old wood.

One afternoon, coming back from a walk, Eleanor stopped short and pointed beneath the porch. A dented metal box sat pushed up against the foundation, half buried in sand and leaves. Hugh crouched to look at it. They talked about crawling under there someday to see what was inside, then went in, leaving the box where it was—as if it had been waiting a long time and could wait a little longer.

Most days, Eleanor took Teeny to the beach while Hugh was at work. Sometimes Doris came too. They crossed the street in bathing suits and thin cover-up robes, carrying a blanket, a bucket and shovel, and a book Eleanor rarely read past the same page. The ocean was green and steady. The waves came in the same way, again and again. Teeny sat in the sand, filling her bucket and dumping it out, certain this was important work.

On Sundays Hugh stayed home. Teeny knew the rhythm of those afternoons. Hugh sat with the newspaper folded just right, working the crossword with a squared-off carpenter's pencil. He sharpened it carefully with his penknife, shaving the wood down to a clean edge. The pencil never rolled when he set it on the table. Teeny watched the knife flash and disappear, then waited for it to come back.

One Sunday, after the puzzle was finished, Eleanor said it was time to look under the porch.

Hugh pulled the metal box out easily. It was lighter than it looked, and the lid opened without a fight. Inside, wrapped in yellowed newspaper, was a framed picture.

It was a pastel painting of the ocean. There was a lighthouse in the distance and a few seagulls caught midair. The frame was plain white wood, worn soft at the corners. At first it seemed simple. But the longer Eleanor stood there, the more the picture changed. The water moved. The sky held weather. Teeny felt something in it too, though she didn't know what—only that it was hard to look away.

They realized the painting showed the view from their own porch: the curve of the shore, the stretch of beach, Buckroe exactly as it was.

Hugh looked closely at the lower right-hand corner.

"Eve M. Allen, '35."

They imagined her standing where they stood, looking out at the same water, deciding to paint it. She must have lived there long before. Eleanor wrapped the picture back up, then unwrapped it again.

They decided to keep it.

They didn't own much—no real furniture, no extras, nothing they couldn't fit into the car if they had to leave. Which they often did. The painting was small, ten inches by fifteen with the frame. It became the only piece of original art they owned. When they moved, it came down from the wall, wrapped in paper, and went with them.

The beach in front of their house was quiet, but farther up the shore was an amusement park. The lighthouse in the painting wasn't real after all. It belonged to the park—a decorative promise rather than a warning.

Hugh and Teeny loved amusement parks. Eleanor liked them well enough, though she only ever rode the carousel, slow and elaborate, its painted horses rising and falling with dignity. Hugh and Teeny preferred the roller coaster. Hugh held Teeny tight as the car climbed and dropped, the ocean flashing past in pieces.

Wherever they lived after that, the painting found a place on the wall. Teeny grew up seeing it there, steady and unmoving. Eleanor sometimes stood in front of it, thinking about Eve Allen—about seeing something ordinary every day and deciding it was worth carrying with you.

The ocean in the picture never changed. Everything else did.

7   Everybody Smoked

Everybody smoked cigarettes.

Hugh smoked. Eleanor smoked. Doris and Leroy smoked. The bars where they ate and drank were full of smoke, the air blue and hanging low. Even the doctor smoked.

When Eleanor brought Teeny to the hospital clinic again because her chest hurt and she wouldn't stop coughing, the doctor coughed too. He asked Eleanor if she smoked.

"Yes," Eleanor said.

"So do I," he said. "Bad habit."

Teeny sat very still while he listened to her chest. The cold circle pressed hard against her skin. When she breathed in, her chest rattled. It hurt. The doctor frowned and said he didn't like the way her lungs sounded.

After that, Teeny remembered nothing.

She woke in a bed with white rails. Her body felt thick and heavy, like it belonged to someone else. Eleanor stood nearby, talking fast.

"The needle was as big as her thigh," she said.

When she saw Teeny's eyes open, she hurried over and bent close.

Hugh stood at the foot of the bed for a moment, then turned and left the room. He said he was going to have a smoke. Eleanor didn't stop him.

Hugh had once buried a baby. It had been winter, the ground frozen, and he'd dug it himself. Family cemetery. Teeny heard Hugh and Eleanor talk about it late at night. She remembered because there was a baby in the story. Hugh Jr. had lived only a few hours. That was before Eleanor. Before Teeny. Hugh didn't say much about it.

There were other stories. Hugh's mother left when he and Leroy were still small. An older brother died as a child, in a hunting accident. After that, Hugh's people stopped expecting things to turn out right.

Eleanor had her own history. She was from Baltimore. She had been married before. She had children. The youngest died as a baby. When Eleanor came home from the hospital after that death, she found her then-husband in bed with another woman. She left him. She did not take the children with her.

These were things said plainly, as if they explained something.

When Hugh and Eleanor met, they recognized something familiar in each other. Loss. Leaving. The way certain things never really stopped happening.

When Teeny got sick, Eleanor watched her closely, counting breaths, listening for changes. She hovered. Hugh went quiet. He stepped back.

Teeny didn't understand any of this. She only knew that when her chest hurt and the air felt thick, everyone moved carefully around her, as if something might break.

8   Velvet Coat

Hugh and Eleanor didn't own much. Hugh didn't like being weighed down by things. Still, he made decent money as a carpenter, and when he didn't spend it at the bar, he handed Eleanor cash for food, clothes, whatever she and Teeny needed.

Hugh dressed for work and little else. Khaki pants, khaki shirt, khaki cap—every day the same, like a uniform. A wide black leather belt and engineer boots that some would call motorcycle boots. He had the kind of looks men didn't have to think about: dark wavy hair, pale blue eyes, a body shaped by labor. For funerals or the occasional dressy night out, he owned one suit, one white shirt, one tie, one pair of dress shoes. When Eleanor dragged him to church, he wore them then, too.

Eleanor liked clothes. She had the taste of the family that had disowned her and never let her forget it. Her grandmother—Araminta "Minty" Hunter Deveraux Van Cleve—had many fine things, but made certain Eleanor would inherit nothing at all.

Eleanor was nearly as tall as Hugh, slim, with a soft hourglass shape and a face that seemed untouched by weather or worry. Hugh liked to say she looked like Hedy Lamarr, and if you squinted just right, you could see it.

They lived in circumstances her family would have disapproved of, and Eleanor corrected this the way she knew how. She dressed Teeny beautifully. Like a doll. She believed clothes opened doors. She believed beauty was currency. And she knew that when it came time to pack the car again, clothes were one thing Hugh wouldn't argue about bringing along.

One afternoon she took Teeny shopping and bought her a silk velvet coat, which cost nearly half of Hugh's weekly pay. Eleanor had saved for weeks and told herself it was fair—he spent his money at the bar, after all—and besides, her daughter would never be taken for low class. Not if Eleanor had anything to say about it.

The coat was red, trimmed with satin piping. Eleanor buttoned Teeny into it, smoothed her hair, fixed her smile. Then she turned the child toward Hugh.

"Doesn't she look like Mrs. Asterbilt's pet pup?" she said.

Hugh thought it was a foolish waste of money. But Eleanor was smiling, and Teeny stood there in the red velvet, solemn and small, and Hugh couldn't bring himself to say a word.

9   Haircut

Hugh and Leroy had worked all day at the construction site—Hugh driving nails, Leroy working with heavy chains and pulleys on the shipyard project they both belonged to. The brothers almost always worked for the same large construction company, often on the same job. It was a time when roads and bridges were rising everywhere, and men from the Appalachian hills traveled into the mid-Atlantic cities to build them. The work was hard and steady, and the pay felt good to men who had grown up with very little. They did not take their jobs for granted.

On Monday evenings, after stopping into the corner bar for a quick drink, Hugh and Leroy went back to their apartments, washed the grit from their hands and faces, and sat down to supper with their wives. Just before 7:30, everyone gathered in Hugh and Eleanor's living room to watch *The Adventures of Robin Hood.*

The lights were low, the television screen flickering blue and white. Hugh, Eleanor, Leroy, and Doris sat quietly, caught up in the story—Robin Hood and his men slipping through the forest, stealing from the rich, giving to the poor. The adults leaned forward without realizing it

Teeny sat nearby in her small rocking chair, the one Hugh had made for her out of oak. It was sturdy and plain, carefully fitted together, not rushed. She rocked gently, not really watching the television. She talked softly to herself and to her dolls, arranging them on her lap.

She had been cutting out paper dolls, carefully separating dresses and coats with the small round-tipped scissors Eleanor kept for her. Lately, Teeny had been thinking about hair. Eleanor and Doris talked about hair often. Hair mattered. Eleanor had told her once, seriously, that she had a long face and needed bangs to cover her forehead. Teeny stored that away.

She knew exactly what tool was needed.

Without standing up, without making a fuss, she asked if she could cut her hair. One of the adults waved a hand and said "Okay," eyes still fixed on the screen.

Teeny leaned forward in her chair and began. She cut straight across first, then trimmed the sides, carefully and confidently, without a mirror and without hesitation. When she finished, she felt satisfied. This was something she had done herself.

She stood up.

"See? I did it."

The table lamp snapped on. Eleanor looked at her and screamed.

"What have you done?"

Teeny froze. She had thought Eleanor would be impressed. Hugh, Leroy, and Doris pressed their lips together, trying not to laugh, and Teeny understood right away she was not going to be spanked—but Eleanor was truly upset.

"It's hair," Hugh said, shaking his head, a smile breaking through. "It'll grow back."

Eleanor fluttered around the room, already planning.

"I'll try to fix it tomorrow," she said.

Then she turned to Teeny, her face tight, and announced it was bedtime.

In the bedroom, Eleanor helped her into her pajamas, scowling as she worked. Teeny stayed quiet. She did not cry. She had done something important, even if no one else could see it yet.

10 Sawdust

Eleanor, Hugh, Leroy and Doris sat at a square table near the back. An extra chair was pulled close to Eleanor for Teeny. The table was crowded with things: two ashtrays mounded with cigarette butts, plates holding the last scraps of food, beer bottles sweating onto paper coasters, half-empty glasses. In front of Eleanor and Teeny were Cokes with thin cocktail straws. The floor was gritty with sawdust.

Teeny hopped down from her chair again and again to feed nickels into the big chrome jukebox. Each time she chose one song, listened for the click, then ran back to the table, her feet skidding a little on the floor. The jukebox stood against the wall like something important, taller than her, shining.

After a while Uncle Leroy reached into his pocket and handed her a quarter.

"You can pick six songs all at once for a quarter," he said. "Saves you a nickel."

Teeny's eyes widened. A quarter meant six songs. She slid off the chair, clutching it tight, already halfway to the jukebox.

As she climbed down, Eleanor called after her.

"Don't play that Johnnie Ray song. I don't like that crying sound in his voice."

Teeny stopped and turned.

"What should I play?"

"Patty Page," Eleanor said.

"Les Paul and Mary Ford," Doris said at the same time.

The women looked at each other and laughed.

"Okay," Teeny said, and ran off.

The chrome jukebox was beautiful. It gleamed on the outside and glowed from within. Behind the glass, everything showed itself. The forty-five-rpm records stood upright in their carousel, waiting. Teeny watched closely as the machine worked: the metal arm sliding into place, selecting, lifting one record with care. There was a pause—long enough to feel important—then the soft clack as the vinyl dropped onto the turntable. The buttons were stiff, each marked with a letter and a number. You had to press hard and mean it.

She chose her six songs carefully and went back to the table, holding the secret inside her chest. It was hard to sit still while she waited.

Uncle Leroy leaned over and said,

"You play something Betty could dance to?"

He flexed his forearm so the Betty Boop tattoo rippled and danced. Teeny, Doris and Hugh laughed. Eleanor smiled, just a little.

Then the jukebox blared to life. Johnnie Ray's voice filled the room, singing "Cry." For a second there was silence. Then everyone laughed.

11   Church

Eleanor went to church. She went to whatever nice-looking Protestant
church was closest to wherever they happened to be living at the time.
In Eleanor's mind, church was part of what decent people did. Putting on
her best clothes, dressing Teeny up, and walking into a church on Sunday
made Eleanor feel as though things were in order.

Most nights Eleanor read the Bible out loud to Teeny before bed. Teeny
listened to the stories and asked questions when they didn't make sense.
Eleanor always had an answer. Sometimes the answers were about how things
used to be. Sometimes they were about what people were trying to say. Teeny
learned that the stories weren't exactly true in the way other things were true.

Easter mattered more than other Sundays. Every year Teeny got a
new outfit: a dress, a hat, gloves, a little purse, and a light coat meant only
for special occasions. Eleanor curled Teeny's hair by rolling it wet into
small plastic curlers and leaving them there until it dried. The curlers hurt.
Eleanor complained that Teeny's hair wouldn't hold a curl.

On holidays Eleanor pushed Hugh, and sometimes Leroy and Doris,
to come to church too. This year Teeny was four, and they all went. There
was singing and a sermon and the collection. Then the man at the pulpit said,
"Now let's bring all the little girls up front to show their pretty new dresses."

Teeny went up with the other children. She didn't know any of
them. She stood still until it was over and then ran back to the pew where
her family was sitting.

Afterward they walked home. Eleanor, Hugh, Leroy, and Doris talked the whole way about how awful it was. They said clothes had nothing
to do with Jesus. They said it was wrong. Eleanor and Hugh said it was
especially bad for children who didn't have new things to wear. Teeny
thought that made sense.

After that, every Easter was the same. Teeny still got a new outfit.
Eleanor still took her to whatever nice-looking Protestant church was nearby.
There was always singing, a sermon, and the collection. Eleanor still read
the Bible at night. Teeny still asked questions when things didn't add up
and learned that things having to do with church were not always what
they appeared to be.

12 You'd Better Watch Out

The radio in the kitchen played Christmas songs while Eleanor ironed. The apartment smelled like hot metal and starch. Eleanor was in a good mood. She sang along, off-key and cheerful, smoothing shirts flat as if she were putting things in order.

When Eddy Arnold's voice came on—You'd better watch out, you'd better not cry—Eleanor wagged her finger at Teeny and sang directly to her, smiling. Teeny felt something drop hard inside her. She stopped what she was doing and watched Eleanor's mouth form the words.

He sees you when you're sleeping.

Eleanor went on, enjoying herself. She shook her finger again.

He knows when you're awake.

Teeny's face tightened. She did not understand how anyone could sing something like that and laugh. By the time Eleanor reached so be good for goodness' sake, Teeny burst into tears. It felt as if something had found her and would not look away.

Eleanor startled and laughed at the same time. "What's wrong? I'm only playing."

Teeny said she didn't like the song. Eleanor dismissed it easily, the way she dismissed most things Teeny objected to. "Don't worry," she said. "Santa Claus will bring you presents." Then she turned back to the ironing, and Teeny went into the other room alone.

That night, not long after Teeny fell asleep, Eleanor heard screaming. Teeny was shaking and holding on to her stuffed rabbit. She could barely speak. She said there was a man watching her. A man looking in the windows.

Eleanor checked the window, annoyed now, and asked if Teeny had had a bad dream. It took a few minutes before she understood. When she did, she laughed. Just a little. That made Teeny furious. Being laughed at felt worse than being watched.

Hugh came to the door, irritated by the noise. Eleanor explained. Hugh snorted. "For Christ's sake. Just tell her."

Eleanor hesitated. "She's only four."

"She's old enough," Hugh said. "Tell her."

So Eleanor told her. She said Santa Claus wasn't real. He was just a story people made up. No one was watching. No one was coming through the windows. Then she added that Teeny must not tell the other children, because they still believed, and it wouldn't be nice to ruin it for them.

The relief came all at once, followed immediately by something colder. Teeny felt stupid for having been scared. Stupider still that grownups had let her be scared. She decided the whole thing was ridiculous.

She still loved Christmas—the lights, the music, the way Eleanor softened for a few weeks—and she kept the secret carefully. She watched other children talk about Santa with solemn certainty and said nothing. As the years went on, she was amazed at how old some of them were when they finally stopped believing.

13   Scranton

Every day was different. Some days there was plenty—too much, even. There was playing and talking and ice cream, walking until Teeny's legs felt rubbery, learning things she didn't yet have names for. When Hugh was working steady and Leroy and Doris were close by, the evenings filled up with sound. The adults laughed and slapped down cards, smoked cigarettes, drank beer. The room felt looser then. Eleanor was calmer, but the calm never went all the way through. There was always a tight line running underneath it.

Eleanor was the center of Teeny's world. Teeny felt Eleanor's eyes on her all the time, measuring, watching, noticing everything.

No matter what kind of day came before, mornings were always the same. Teeny woke to Hugh coughing—deep, tearing coughs that shook the walls—followed by the wet, grinding sound of him spitting phlegm and blood into the kitchen sink. The sink noise bothered her more than the coughing. It went on too long. Eleanor never commented. Hugh's cough was just there, like the table or the stove.

It was a smoker's cough mixed with the sickness that came after drinking too much beer. Hugh's muscles ached from hard work, his head hurt, his stomach burned. By morning he was sharp-edged and impatient, and everyone moved around him carefully.

Leroy and Doris were still nearby then, but Doris coughed more every day and seemed to shrink inside her clothes. Eleanor said, "Doris is so skinny a stiff wind could blow her away." Leroy had never said much, and now he said even less. The shipyard job was ending. No one said it out loud, but Teeny felt it pressing in, the way the air changed before a storm.

Soon they were packing again. Not just across town this time. The five of them drove north in two cars filled to the roof. They landed in Scranton, Pennsylvania. The town had flooded not long before, and the water from the faucets wasn't safe to drink. Leroy went out to look for work. Doris stayed inside, too sick to move much.

Eleanor took Teeny with her and Hugh up the mountain, where a pipe stuck straight out of the rocks and ran with clean water. They brought gallon jugs and waited their turn with other people from town, filling bottle after bottle. The air was damp and heavy. Normally Teeny would have liked this—walking, waiting, watching water spill and splash—but everyone was quiet. That quiet made her quieter too.

That night Hugh and Leroy talked low and serious. They told Eleanor and Doris they were all leaving for Baltimore the next morning. Teeny watched Eleanor's face change—hope passing through it, then something darker right behind. Teeny had been told that she was born in Baltimore, but didn't remember it. She knew that things were about to be different.

Hugh had adhesive tape wrapped around his ribs. He said that it was pleurisy and he couldn't work. When he had his coughing fits in the morning, everything hurt worse. The coughing shook his whole body, and the pain climbed up into his face until it looked tight and strange, like it didn't belong to him anymore.

Eleanor sat in the rocking chair with a hot water bottle pressed to her stomach. The chair was close to the bed and the stove, all of it crowded into one small room. Teeny played on the bed, careful not to bounce too hard. The apartment stayed dark even during the day. The windows didn't let in much light, and the light that did come through looked tired, like it wanted to lie back down.

Teeny didn't know what pleurisy was and she didn't know why her mother's stomach hurt all the time either. She knew she was supposed to be quiet. She knew she was supposed to read her books and not ask questions. Quiet felt safer.

Leroy and Doris had come with them to Baltimore, but they lived farther away now. Hugh and Eleanor talked in low voices about Doris maybe going in the sanitarium and about something called TB. They worried about how Leroy would manage on his own. Teeny listened from the bed, the words floating above her like dust. They didn't settle into anything she could hold.

A few days later, the three of them packed the car again.

"Put whatever you want to keep in your little red suitcase," Eleanor said.

The suitcase belonged to Teeny. It was where any of her things that she didn't want to leave behind went. She got to keep it in the car with her when they traveled. It was red with black checks, with a clear Bakelite handle and brass trim, just the right size for her hands. She chose some books and a few toys and carried the suitcase out herself, a small pillow tucked under her arm.

Once the car was packed and everyone was inside, Teeny felt safe again. Cars meant going somewhere else. Going somewhere else usually meant things would be better, or at least different.

They drove north and west, back to western Pennsylvania, to see

Hugh's older sister.

"We're going to see your Aunt Addie," Eleanor said brightly, the way she talked to dogs and cats.

"Who's Aunt Addie?" Teeny asked.

"She's your father's sister," Eleanor said. "She raised him. She's like his mother."

Hugh said nothing and kept his eyes on the road.

Addie was happy to see Hugh and called him baby brother over and over. She touched his arm when she said it, as if he might drift away. Eleanor smoked constantly and began grinding her teeth without seeming to notice. When Teeny talked too much or asked questions, she could feel Addie watching her, sharp and steady.

"That kid's got a smart mouth on her," Addie said to Hugh, not smiling.

Teeny met Addie's grown daughters while they were there—Aunt Ramona and Aunt Evangeline. Evangeline lived with Addie. She reminded Teeny of Doris, only not as kind. Everyone called her Boots, though Teeny couldn't understand why, since she didn't wear boots.

On the third day Aunt Ramona came to visit Hugh. They acted like siblings, both of them careful around Addie, both of them giving way to her. When Ramona walked into a room, it felt different. She talked with her whole face. Her eyes seemed to speak before her mouth did. When she laughed, it sounded like she knew something no one else did. Teeny liked watching her, but she wasn't sure she trusted her.

There wasn't much to do there except watch Addie cook. She liked making a lot of food and putting it on the table, and Hugh praised her cooking every time. They told Teeny that Ramona had a little girl who was still a baby and that she would meet her someday. Someday felt very far away.

It seemed that whatever Eleanor and Hugh thought they would find there was missing. Teeny could feel it, the way you feel when a room looks right but doesn't feel right, and you don't know why.

One night, after they had been there for a week and Teeny had fallen asleep, Hugh and Eleanor talked in whispers that sounded angry. Even quiet, the words felt sharp, like they could cut through sleep.

By morning, they were packing the car again.

The car was packed to the roof. Teeny sat in the front seat between Eleanor and Hugh, perched on her suitcase so she could see out the windshield, putting her level with Eleanor and Hugh. Outside, the moon hung low and round, too big to be real.

They were going fast over a bridge when Hugh tipped his head toward the window. Eleanor broke the quiet.

"Look, Teeny. That's the Allegheny River."

Teeny watched the moon wobble in the dark water. She knew the word Allegheny from a song she had heard on a jukebox. She held the picture in her mind for a moment, then said, "So is that the Allegheny Moon?"

Eleanor laughed. Hugh laughed harder. Teeny laughed too, though she didn't know what she had said that was funny. It felt good to be laughed with.

Hugh drove fast, the way he always did. A red flashing light appeared behind them, bright and sudden. A Pennsylvania state trooper pulled the car over. Teeny stayed very still while Hugh handed over his license and the trooper asked questions that didn't seem to have right answers.

The trooper wrote a ticket and said it had to be paid in cash, right then. Eleanor's face went stiff. She held her breath, like she was holding something heavy inside her chest. Hugh argued in a low voice. The trooper waited. Eventually the car pulled back onto the road.

"Bastard got every red cent," Hugh said, watching the road in the rearview mirror.

"That wasn't right," Eleanor said. She was crying now, her voice sharp and thin. "That was a crooked cop."

Teeny listened without speaking. She knew something bad had happened, even if she didn't know what it was. After a while, her eyes closed. She slept on Eleanor's lap, the suitcase on the floor under Eleanor's feet, Hugh driving without a word.

When they reached Baltimore, it was still dark. They parked on a block of big old houses, all cut up into apartments. Sitting in the car, Hugh and Eleanor talked quietly, the anger still there.

"I have an idea," Eleanor said. "You stay here, Hugh."

She got out and pulled the small television from the back seat. It had a silver antenna that slid up from the top. Eleanor took Teeny's hand and lifted the TV with the other. "Don't talk," she said. "Just stand there."

They climbed marble steps to a door with a sign in the window. Eleanor knocked. A man answered. Eleanor told him she and her daughter needed a place to stay but didn't have any money. There was a long story about why there was no cash. She asked if he would take the television instead, just for a few days, until she could get some money together.

The man hesitated. He looked at the TV. He looked at Teeny. Finally, he nodded. Eleanor added that her husband would be staying too and would be there soon. The man's mouth tightened, but he let them in and handed her a key.

Teeny followed Eleanor inside, still holding her hand. Outside, in the car, Hugh watched the dawn break.

Teeny wore one of her Sunday dresses, the one that made Eleanor's mouth press into a careful line while she buttoned it. The dress meant something important was going to happen. Teeny felt it in her stomach—tight and jumpy at the same time. She was going to meet the other children. Eleanor's children from before. Teeny didn't know exactly what that meant, only that it meant she was supposed to stand still and behave.

Hugh drove without talking. He let them out at a gas station on a corner where the sidewalk buckled and the houses leaned toward the street like they were tired of standing up. The garage doors were open and the air smelled sharp and oily. Eleanor smoothed Teeny's hair with a hand that didn't stop moving. They were going to wait here, Eleanor said. Hugh would come back later. He nodded once and drove away.

Teeny wondered why they were at a gas station. She was about to ask, when a tall man came through the garage door, wiping his hands on a rag. He wore blue coveralls and had a smile that didn't reach his eyes. He looked Eleanor up and down and said, "So you're here to see the kids."

Eleanor said yes. They talked like people who knew each other too well and didn't want to say it. The man looked down at Teeny. "So, this is his kid?"

Eleanor's hand tightened. "Teeny," she said, "this is Ray Parks. This is his garage." She pointed to the sign—Ray's Gas and Garage—she knew Teeny could read it, even if Ray didn't. Teeny looked at Ray and then looked away. She didn't like how he looked at her, like she was a thing someone had left behind.

They walked half a block to a small white house with weeds taller than the steps. The porch sagged in the middle, and the screen door hung loose, flapping when Ray pushed it open. Inside, a baby cried from near the door, its diaper dark and swollen. The sound filled the room and didn't stop.

"Gladys," Ray yelled toward the back, already turning away. "Eleanor's here to see the kids."

A small woman with stringy blonde hair came out of the kitchen. She looked tired, like she had forgotten something important and couldn't remember what. "They're outside," she said, as if that explained everything.

Teeny didn't let go of Eleanor's hand. The house smelled wrong. There were things everywhere—on the floor, on the chairs, on the walls. As they turned back toward the door, Eleanor pulled Teeny short. "Watch it," she said sharply.

Teeny looked down. There was poop on the floor. She froze, afraid of stepping in it, afraid of breathing. She had never been anywhere like this before, and she wanted very badly to be somewhere else.

Outside, a boy came running around the side of the house. He was loud and fast and smiling, like he had been waiting just for them. "Hi, Teeny!" he said, as if her name already belonged to him.

She smiled back without thinking. She liked him right away.

"This is your big brother Billy," Eleanor said.

Billy cupped his hands around his mouth and shouted toward a car parked out front. "Bucky! Come here!"

A tall, skinny teenager got out of the car slowly. He moved like everything was heavier than it should be. He had sad blue eyes and looked mostly at his shoes. Billy talked for him—about a car he was going to get, an old one from the garage, something Bucky could fix and keep. Eleanor said, "Bucky, this is your little sister Teeny."

Bucky nodded. Teeny felt sorry for him, though she didn't know why.

"Where's Maggie?" Eleanor asked.

"Down the corner," Bucky said. "She'll be up in a minute."

Then Maggie appeared, walking up the street like she was arriving somewhere she already owned. She looked like a grown-up lady, not like a girl. Her ponytail bounced, her skirt hugged her legs, and the jacket she wore was too big on purpose. She had lipstick on and a ring hanging from a chain at her neck. She moved smooth, like the people on television.

"Maggie," Eleanor said, tight again. "This is Teeny."

Teeny stared. Maggie was beautiful. Teeny stood very still, holding Eleanor's hand, trying to understand how someone could be family and a stranger at the same time.

17   Books and Television

Eleanor could turn a cheap furnished apartment into a home in a single day, using only what would fit in the car. She made end tables out of cardboard boxes, hiding them under floor-length tablecloths so they looked intentional. Curtains came from bedsheets. Throw pillows were sewn from old clothes and stuffed with even older ones. Sometimes she painted cabinets or papered walls, even when they would only be there for a few months, or a few weeks.

Teeny watched this closely. She watched how rooms changed once Eleanor touched them. She learned where things should go. She learned that a place could feel right even if it wasn't meant to last. It never occurred to her that this was unusual. She assumed all women could do this. In the same way, she assumed all men could build a wooden toy box, or a table, if one was needed.

She thought all families read together at the kitchen table, each person with a book propped open beside a plate. Eating and reading happened at the same time. In her family, everyone read whenever there was a moment to spare. Hugh and Eleanor had not gone to school past the eighth grade, but that didn't seem to matter. They knew things. They wanted to know more things. They followed whatever caught their interest until it ran out.

Teeny could not remember a time before she could read. She had been very small when words stopped being pictures and became meaning. She asked questions constantly. Sometimes Hugh answered. Sometimes Eleanor did. Sometimes Leroy or Doris. Often, they said, "Look it up."

Eleanor loved the library. In every new place, one of the first things she did was find it. She made sure everyone had a card. They borrowed books from the library, and also owned some books that went with them when they moved.

Everyone in the family made things. Hugh could build almost anything they needed. What he made was solid and useful. He didn't bother with decoration. He didn't carve or polish much. He understood how things went together, and he had the strength to make them hold. Teeny was too small to hammer a nail properly. Hugh once told her that if it took more than three hits to drive a nail all the way in, you were doing it wrong. She remembered this while snapping together her plastic building blocks. She almost always made a house. When the pieces locked into place, she felt the same quiet satisfaction she saw on Hugh's face when he finished something.

They all watched television. Sometimes Teeny watched alone. Sometimes they watched together. Teeny noticed that the families on TV lived differently. Their houses were larger and stayed in the same place. The fathers wore suits and carried briefcases to offices. The mothers wore dresses and pearl necklaces and did not seem to make or fix anything. The children did not read for fun. They did not build things. They did not play cards with their parents.

Teeny understood that television was not real.

18 "Ireland"

When Teeny's father and uncle Leroy talked about going back to the western Pennsylvania hills where they had grown up, they didn't say the name of the place. They said they were going back to Ireland.

Teeny knew they weren't actually going to Ireland. She also knew that when adults agreed on a name like that, it wasn't something you were meant to ask about.

Their father, Joseph, had been called Irish since he was young. After a few beers, he would do an Irish jig—stamping and hopping on kitchen floors, laughing while everyone else laughed harder. His children called him Pap or Irish, depending on the day. They told stories about their grandmother, Irish's mother Agnes Flanagan, who had taught him the dance when he was little. Hugh had described her as "a right bitch" so in Teeny's mind, Agnes was sour-faced and sharp-tongued. It was hard to picture her laughing, or teaching anyone how to dance. Irish had died of a heart attack in 1952 but the family still told stories about him. It felt to Teeny like he was still alive.

At five, Teeny was still small for her age, and her mother still carried her on her hip. They were visiting the place her father came from, near the old Flanagan farm, where the land folded in on itself and the roads narrowed without warning. Her father wanted to stop and see his old friend, Red Callahan.

This was where she learned what a bootlegger was.

This was also where she learned what it meant for a county to be dry.

Her mother said it wasn't a good place to bring a little girl. She didn't drink. She sounded serious when she said this. But they went anyway.

The weather was cold and sharp. They parked along the road and walked toward the house, crossing a wide ditch on a single plank laid across it. Water moved quietly underneath. Her father lifted her without comment. When he was building bridges, he walked high beams without a harness. Here, at Red Callhan's he crossed the slick plank as if it were nothing more than a step between rooms. Teeny looked down once, then pressed her face into his shoulder.

Red Callahan's back door opened straight into the kitchen. The air inside was warm and damp, heavy with smoke. A wooden table held stone crocks filled with clear liquid. Bottles of beer sat among them, pretending to belong. Men crowded close, talking and laughing, their voices low and steady. Cigarette smoke lifted and vanished into the ceiling.

Teeny watched everything.

Her mother stayed near the door. She looked neat and out of place in her perfectly ironed Sunday clothes, her hands worrying each other when Teeny refused to stand beside her. Teeny wanted to be near the table. She wanted to listen. No one told her to move.

When it was time to leave, her father carried her back across the plank. He was just as steady as before. Her mother watched his feet the entire way. When they reached the road, she let out a breath and said, "Hugh, you are part mountain goat."

Teeny had never seen a mountain goat, but she understood that it was a compliment.

The family lived mostly in cities. Sometimes they went to the country for a while, but they never stayed long. They were always moving. There were no vacations, just driving. In some ways, the car felt more like home than any of the places they stopped. Even when they weren't moving to a new place, they went for long rides.

The car was big and heavy on the outside, soft on the inside. It had bench seats and no seat belts. Inside it felt like a separate world, one that floated along while everything else passed by. Time didn't seem to matter there.

In the car, nobody fought.

Sometimes things got exciting. Hugh would press hard on the gas and the engine would growl. Eleanor would grab the handle above the passenger door and shout, "HUGH!" Her voice would go tight and sharp. Teeny loved this part. She would laugh and call out from the back seat, "Faster, Daddy, faster." Hugh would grin and push the car faster still, the speedometer climbing high, the road rushing underneath them. Teeny's stomach would feel light, like it was lifting. Then Hugh would slow the car again, giving in to Eleanor's fear.

They sang together while Hugh drove. Teeny sat in the back seat and sang as loud as she could. "The Bear Went Over the Mountain." She knew every word. Their voices filled the car and bounced off the windows.

Sometimes Teeny rode in the front seat between them. Other times she lay stretched out on the back seat, watching the tops of trees slide past the window until her eyes closed. She could play quiet games or look at her books. The car rocked her to sleep.

There was always a folded paper map in the car. Eleanor opened it wide across her lap, smoothing it with her hands. She traced the roads with her finger, matching them to signs and rivers and towns they passed. When they were close to wherever they planned to stop, she would say, "Time to put your shoes on." Teeny obeyed.

They stopped at gas stations where Hugh would lean out the window and say, "Fill 'er up," to the man in uniform. Sometimes they pulled over instead, and Eleanor and Hugh bent over the map together, talking quietly about where to go next.

Rest stops were patches of dirt and trees beside the road. Sometimes there was a wooden picnic table. They ate food they had brought with them. Hugh pointed out trees and told Teeny their names. He talked about animals that lived nearby, even if none could be seen. If he was in a good mood, he flexed his arm to make the bird tattoo on his bicep flap its wings. Teeny laughed every time.

Sometimes Eleanor took pictures with the small box camera. The film was rolled inside and couldn't touch the light. The pictures would be developed later, sometime far away.

Hugh liked to wander off into the woods. He disappeared between the trees and came back after a while. Sometimes he brought things with him—a deer antler, a rock, an unusual looking pinecone. Eleanor watched the trees while he was gone, fluttery and uneasy, though she seemed to know how long he would be. Teeny didn't question it.

Living in Baltimore was different from other places. It seemed dark inside every apartment they moved to. This newest place was small and set inside a three-story brick building. It always felt a little dim, even during the day. But the best thing wasn't inside at all. It was directly across the street.

The park seemed enormous to Teeny. The sun sparkled on the duck pond and there were squirrels everywhere, birds that hopped and chattered in the trees, swings that went high when Hugh pushed her, and—best of all—a tall building that looked like a pagoda. It had porches stacked one above the other, way up in the air. People used to be allowed to go up there and look out, but not anymore. Teeny asked why. Eleanor said it wasn't safe.

On days when Hugh wasn't working, the three of them crossed the street with a blanket and a packed lunch and sat on the grass. Hugh loved feeding the squirrels. He held peanuts very still until a squirrel trusted him enough to take one from his hand. Sometimes he lay on his back and put the peanut on his chest. If everyone stayed perfectly quiet, the squirrel would climb right onto him. Teeny watched, hardly breathing.

Those afternoons were the best part of the week. Most days Hugh was gone early, working construction on a bridge. Uncle Leroy worked there too. They didn't see Aunt Doris anymore. When Hugh and Eleanor talked about her, their voices dropped low, the words slipping past Teeny like something meant not to be caught.

Eleanor had a job as well. She took the bus downtown to a sewing factory where she made policemen's hats. Eleanor called it a sweatshop.

Teeny went to nursery school. The building faced the park and was only a block and a half from the apartment. Eleanor walked her there in the mornings before catching the bus. The woman in the office wore a uniform and was kind. Each morning she gave every child a vitamin. Teeny asked what the vitamin was for. The woman said it helped keep them healthy. Teeny knew Eleanor liked this.

The nursery school was called the Salvation Army. Teeny asked Eleanor why it was an army. Eleanor said the name came from the Bible and meant helping people and saving souls, not fighting with weapons.

She also explained that the people who ran the nursery school had a church.

There were many other children there. Some days they all went to the park together. Teeny liked being in a place she already knew, but being there with the other children made her more aware of her parents' absence. She did not confuse this feeling with fear. It made the world feel bigger somehow.

The nursery school had shelves of books, puzzles with all their pieces, toys that were put away when you were finished with them, and lunches with chocolate milk. Teeny had always been a picky eater. At home, not eating could cause trouble. Here it did not. Prunes were served in a small bowl. They were brown, cloudy, and wrinkled. Teeny examined them closely and declined. No one commented. She noted this difference.

Nap time took place in a large room filled with small cots. Each child had a blanket. Teeny liked the order of it. Lying there among the others, she allowed herself to sleep, knowing that the people who ran the school were outside the door making sure the children were safe.

In the afternoons, children were picked up one by one. As the room emptied, the sound changed. Teeny was usually one of the last to leave, sometimes the last. The remaining children were allowed to watch television. Teeny liked television, but here it made her feel exposed. She watched the door carefully. She knew Eleanor was working, and she knew how buses functioned, but knowing these things did not make waiting easier.

Eleanor always came. They walked back across the street together, past the park and the pagoda, and into the dim apartment, the door closing behind them.

Hugh and Eleanor liked to take Teeny for rides in the car on weekend afternoons. They would drive without a plan. When they came to a fork in the road, they asked Teeny which way to go. Sometimes they brought food. Sometimes they stopped somewhere to eat.

One afternoon they stopped at a tavern for lunch when there were no other customers yet. The woman behind the bar said she owned the place. Along one wall there was a large birdcage. Inside was a bird about the size of the pigeons Teeny had seen in the park. It had shiny dark feathers and bright yellow legs and beak.

The woman said it was a myna bird. She said it could talk.

Everyone went over to the cage. They waited. The bird looked at them and said, "Man wants more beer!"

Hugh laughed so hard Teeny thought he might choke. Eleanor laughed too. Hugh ordered a beer. Eleanor ordered lunch. Teeny stood close to the cage.

The bird talked some more. It said "Hello." It said "Pretty bird." It said words Teeny knew she wasn't supposed to say. It whistled and squawked and made strange clicking sounds. But it kept coming back to the same thing.

"Man wants more beer!"

They left the tavern laughing and got back into the big green Buick with the round portholes on the side. Teeny climbed into the back seat, Eleanor sat in the front, and Hugh pulled out of the parking lot. Almost immediately, a police car turned on its lights.

Everything in the car went quiet.

The policeman asked Hugh if he had seen the No Left Turn sign. Hugh said he hadn't. He said they were just out driving. The policeman took out his ticket book and a pen. Then he looked at Teeny in the back seat.

"That your little girl?" he asked.

Hugh said yes. Eleanor nodded.

The policeman smiled. He closed the ticket book. "Since she's so cute, I'm going to let you off with just a warning. Looks like today's your lucky day."

Hugh's face lit up. "Yes, Sir!" Eleanor and Teeny waved as they drove away.

One Sunday, Hugh took Eleanor and Teeny to meet a couple who owned a bar near one of his construction jobs. The bar was closed, but the owners were there anyway. They had two boys about Teeny's age. The boys didn't look very interested. They looked almost exactly alike, except one was a little taller. Both were bigger than Teeny, with short blond hair and unfriendly faces.

Teeny would have rather stayed inside with the grownups, but she was expected to go outside and play. The boys led her onto the sidewalk and asked if she wanted to see something they liked to do. Teeny said "okay" and followed.

Between the cracks in the sidewalk there was a small anthill. Ants were everywhere, busy and fast, carrying crumbs someone had dropped. Teeny crouched down to watch.

All at once the boys started stomping. They jumped up and down, yelling and laughing, crushing the ants as fast as they could.

"Take that!" one yelled.

Teeny felt sick. She ran back inside the bar crying. Eleanor told her it was alright. Hugh laughed a little. The boys' parents laughed too. "Boys will be boys," they said.

After that, Teeny stayed right next to Eleanor and wouldn't go back outside. The woman who owned the bar left and came back with an ice cream bar for Teeny. She said Teeny could look around if she wanted and that there was a nice dog who lived there.

Teeny walked toward the back of the bar. A large black dog lay asleep. She thought it looked lonely. She wanted to pet it. She wanted to share her ice cream. She bent down close to the dog's face and held the ice cream near its mouth.

The dog woke suddenly. It snarled and snapped. Its teeth scraped Teeny's lip.

She screamed. She couldn't stop crying. She shook all over. Eleanor rushed over and looked at her mouth. There was only a small scrape. Eleanor said, "You'll be okay," and smoothed Teeny's hair.

Hugh and Eleanor apologized as they said goodbye. Teeny thought it was the bar owners who should have been sorry.

22 Smile

It was dark by the time Eleanor picked Teeny up from the nursery school, and they walked back to the apartment together, Eleanor tired from her job at the sewing factory, Teeny keeping pace beside her.

Hugh was not around much, except in the mornings, when Teeny heard him coughing and gagging and spitting before he left for work. She would pretend to still be asleep so she wouldn't get in the way and be yelled at.

As soon as Hugh left, Teeny put on the clothes Eleanor had laid out the night before. They hurried out of the apartment, and as Eleanor buttoned Teeny's coat and settled her hat on her head, she said, as she always did, "Remember, nobody loves you but me."

Eleanor smiled when she said it.

Teeny did not answer.

At night, Teeny could hear Eleanor crying. She didn't know how to help and felt small and useless. Hugh was gone most evenings, and when he was there, he slept on the floor. He slept so hard that nothing could wake him, but Eleanor still reminded Teeny to be quiet.

There was going to be a Christmas pageant at the nursery school, and Teeny was supposed to sing with the other children. Eleanor made sure she had something new to wear.

The skirt was a very full circle made of gray felt. It stuck out far when Teeny turned. On the front were black kittens embroidered in thread. You could tell they were circus cats because one wore a ballet tutu and another swung from a trapeze. Teeny loved the skirt. When she put it on, she felt more like herself.

Eleanor dressed her carefully, brushing her shiny dark hair and fastening it with barrettes shaped like circus elephants, one on each side. When they were ready, Eleanor took Teeny by the hand and said to Hugh, "I expect we'll see you and Leroy there."

"Yeah, yeah," Hugh said. "See you later."

The Salvation Army nursery school was warm and bright and busy. A huge Christmas tree stood in the middle of the room, covered in shiny lights and tinsel. Steps had been set up beside it where the children would line up to sing. There were wrapped packages under the tree with ribbons and bows.

A man with a big camera was taking pictures. Each time he pressed the button, a flashbulb went off. Teeny noticed that before their pictures were taken, each child was put into a red circular cape with a very large white bow. The capes covered up everyone's clothes.

Teeny did not like the capes. She especially did not like that they hid her skirt.

Eleanor used the high voice she saved for cats and dogs. "Doesn't everybody look cute," she said, smiling too hard.

Teeny did not think they looked cute at all. When it was her turn, they put the cape on her and told her to smile. Teeny would not smile while she was being covered up. She made her hands into tight fists and held her arms stiff at her sides. She looked at Eleanor and then at the man with the camera.

"Smile, honey," the man said.

"Teeny," Eleanor said, her own smile stretched thin, "smile so the man can take your picture."

Teeny did not smile. The man took the picture anyway.

Teeny could feel Eleanor's unhappiness, but everything went on as planned. Teeny stood with the other children in the choir, still wearing the ugly cape with the big bow, and sang the songs they had practiced. She sang carefully and correctly.

Hugh and Leroy showed up to watch. They did not act like the other people there. They laughed too loud and shifted their feet, as if they didn't know where to stand. They had been drinking.

As soon as Teeny's part was over, Eleanor told the nursery school woman that they had to leave. Outside, Leroy looked ashamed. Hugh laughed about how Teeny wouldn't smile for the picture or the singing, like it was a trick she had done on purpose.

Eleanor did not smile. At the door to the building, Hugh said he and Leroy were going back to the bar for a while and the two men walked away. Eleanor took Teeny's hand and went inside. She did not say anything, and her face stayed set the whole way up the stairs.

23   The Outhouse

In March they moved to the country. It was the first time Teeny, Eleanor, and Hugh had lived alone in a whole house with no other adults nearby. There was a big yard. The nearest neighbor had a farm with chickens and cornfields.

The house was a small two-bedroom bungalow that needed work. There was no indoor bathroom and no heat, but some old furniture had been left behind. Hugh built an outhouse. He had built outhouses when he was young. Where he grew up, outhouses were normal.

He also built wooden steps up to the back door and fixed the screen.

Out there, between Baltimore and Annapolis, an outhouse wasn't normal, but it was necessary. Eleanor quit her job at the sewing factory. Hugh still went to work most days. The weather stayed cold, so they used a space heater and wore sweaters. Teeny could still bathe in the kitchen sink.

Hugh seemed more relaxed than he had been in Baltimore.

Eleanor told herself this was a choice. She remembered living with her grandparents on the Bush River one summer, after her parents divorced and tried to believe this was the same kind of thing. She said it would be good for Teeny. Still, she never quite settled. She moved through the house carefully, as if she were afraid of breaking something.

They told Teeny how lucky she was to live in the country and how great it would be to have animals. They got a young collie, tri-colored and not fully grown. Teeny named the dog Elvis, even though it was a girl. She knew the song "Hound Dog" from jukeboxes in bars and thought it was the right name for a dog.

They planted a big garden. Teeny helped put the seeds in the ground. When bugs showed up on the potato plants, it was Teeny's job to knock them into a tin can with kerosene using a stick. It was disgusting, but she liked having a job to do.

There was an old chicken coop behind the house, but no chickens. Hugh built a rabbit hutch onto it, and Teeny got a black rabbit named Crusader. Hugh hung a wooden swing from the big oak tree in the yard. There was a tire swing, too.

The outhouse was clean and smelled like fresh wood. It had a real toilet seat and a little step stool for Teeny to climb up. Hugh left detective magazines there. Eleanor left Family Circle.

It was strange to leave the house to use the bathroom, and stranger still that you couldn't wash your hands until you went back inside, but it wasn't as bad as Teeny had thought it would be.

No one looked up to see the wasp nest tucked into the corner near the roof.

One afternoon, Teeny went into the outhouse and was stung between the eyes. She screamed. Eleanor came running and was stung, too.

Eleanor knew right away what that meant. She was allergic. Hugh wasn't home. They didn't know the neighbors. She grabbed Teeny and ran for the house, trying to get them both inside and to the telephone.

The ambulance came quickly and took them to the emergency room. They both got shots. Eleanor's eyes had been swollen shut, but by the time they were sent home she could see again. She kept asking if Teeny was all right.

That night, Eleanor made fried chicken and told Hugh what had happened. Hugh said Eleanor should have a car in case something else went wrong while he was away.

A few days later, an old black Studebaker appeared in the yard. It was Eleanor's car. Teeny had never seen Eleanor drive before and thought it was exciting.

Not long after that, Eleanor took Teeny out in the car to go shopping. The big car rolled fast down Mountain Road. Eleanor pressed the brake and felt nothing happen. She pressed it again.

The brakes didn't work.

She told Teeny to sit down and hold on. Eleanor pulled the emergency brake with her left hand, but the car kept going. She downshifted, and that slowed it some. At the bottom of the hill, she saw a wide gravel parking lot bordered with logs. She steered into it and drove the car in large circles until it struck one of the logs with a hard bump.

The car stopped. No one was hurt.

After that, Eleanor was not sure she really wanted a car.

Teeny had her sixth birthday party in the country. She wore an orange-and-white striped dress she loved. And her pearls—one strand, not three like Eleanor's. She had dress shoes that were not corrective shoes, and socks with lace at the cuffs. Everything was right except the straps across the shoes, with their small buckles. Straps were for babies.

She took the shoes to Hugh and asked if he would cut the straps off. He said he could, then glanced up as Eleanor came into the room. Eleanor asked what was happening. Teeny told her Hugh was fixing the shoes so they wouldn't look like baby shoes. Eleanor made a face. Hugh shrugged.

"Alright?"

Eleanor sighed. "I don't have a good argument why not."

Hugh cut the straps. Teeny clapped and put the shoes on immediately. They were just right.

Hugh and Eleanor twisted long balloons into animal shapes. Teeny decided it was going to be a very good day.

Eleanor had invited the children from the farm next door. Teeny didn't know them, but it was outside, and she liked the idea of other children being there. None of them were her age. There was a quiet boy of about eight in overalls with no shirt. He ate a lot and popped balloons and wouldn't wear a party hat. There was a very fat little boy, maybe two, who talked so poorly Teeny could hardly understand him. There was one girl, about three, in a pretty dress. She let her mother put a party hat on her but touched everything before she ate it.

They told Teeny the girl was blind because her mother had had the measles. Teeny didn't know how that worked. She felt sorry for her anyway. There were candles on the cake. People sang. Teeny made a wish. They ate hot dogs, cake, and ice cream at the picnic table Hugh had built.

Afterward, the children invited Teeny to see their farm. There were chickens and a large white rooster. They said the chickens laid eggs in different colors. Teeny walked closer to the rooster.

"Watch out," an adult said. "He can be mean." The rooster jumped on her back, dug in his claws, and pecked at her head. Teeny screamed.

The adults ran and chased the rooster away. She wanted to go home.

She never asked to visit the farm again. All summer she played by herself. She ran with her dog. She swung on her swing. She petted her rabbit.

Sometimes the older boy and his friends rode past on their bicycles and threw rocks at Elvis. Elvis barked and chased them. One day Elvis ran off and didn't come back for hours. Eleanor found her later on the road and dragged her home by the collar. After that, things seemed quiet.

They weren't.

An angry man came to the door and shouted that the dog had been killing his chickens. Eleanor apologized. The man said he would call the pound. A few days later the sheriff came with a man holding a long pole with a wire loop. They said they were taking the dog. Teeny screamed. Eleanor asked if there was anything she could do. The men said no.

Elvis fought. The wire went around her neck. They dragged her to a truck with a closed back and slammed the door. The truck drove away. Teeny cried for a long time. She asked if Elvis would come back.

"No," Eleanor said. "She's not ever coming back."

PART TWO

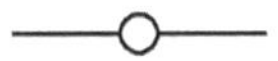

"Claire?" the teacher called. A pause. "Claire?" a little louder. Then, finally, "Is Claire Young here?" Teeny looked up from her book. "Yes, I'm here."

The book was *On Cherry Street,* handed to every child with the announcement that this year, they would learn to read. Teeny had been told her real name was Claire, but she almost never heard it spoken out loud. At home, she was always Teeny. Hugh had called her Teeny from the time she was born and it stuck.

Other names had come and gone. Once, when she was two, Eleanor took her to a new doctor. "What's your name, little girl?" he asked. Teeny stared. "What does your mommy call you?" he tried again. "Little brat. Little beast. Little monster," she said. The doctor laughed. Eleanor blushed. "Her name is Claire," she explained. "But we call her Teeny."

At six she sat at a wobbly desk in a temporary classroom that smelled like plywood and cleaning supplies. Her red plaid bookbag with black straps and silver buckles stood beside her chair. Every child had the same book. The same desk. The teacher said by June they would all be able to read it, even if the words did not make sense yet.

Claire began at the first page. By the time the teacher reached the end of roll call, she had finished the book. She closed it and placed both hands flat on the cover. The room was still on the first chapter.

She kept them there for a minute. Then she opened it again.

She did not know the children around her. Some turned in their seats. Most kept their eyes on the teacher. They had been to kindergarten. She had not.

She tried to follow along. It was too slow. She turned the pages and looked down.

The floor was bare linoleum. The air carried the sharp, clean smell of something recently mopped. In her bookbag, a metal lunch box waited: peanut butter and jelly on white bread, a pear, Tastykake chocolate cupcakes. Some days it would be American cheese instead, an apple in place of the pear.

When the bell rang, she walked down the grassy hill toward home. Across the street stood the housing projects.

It was Eleanor, Billy, Bucky, and Teeny. Hugh was not there.

26   Brooklyn Homes

The squat brick buildings all looked the same. Each had six identical doors
and three sets of concrete steps, two families to a stoop, with a shallow
portico over each one. Four buildings faced a shared courtyard. There were
nearly 500 units altogether, identical from the outside and nearly so inside.

Upstairs were two small bedrooms and a bathroom. Downstairs
were the living room and the kitchen. Eleanor took the smaller bedroom.
The larger one held a set of bunk beds for Teeny and Billy, and Bucky slept
on a cot in the same room.

Eleanor worked at the sewing factory downtown from seven in the
morning until five, five days a week. Some evenings and Saturdays she
tended bar. No matter how much she worked, there was never enough
money. She would sit at the table with the bills spread out and ask Teeny
which ones to pay and which ones to let pile up until next month. She
called it robbing Peter to pay Paul.

Teeny tried to think carefully. The electric bill or the phone bill.
Food or the shoes Billy needed. It felt important to get it right.

Teeny was often sick and missed school. Billy hated school and was
always happy to stay home with her. He made pancakes from Bisquick,
milk, and an egg, pouring the batter into the pan in letters so it spelled
her name. At lunchtime he heated up a can of Campbell's chicken noodle
soup and then laughed and told her the noodles were worms.
Billy was full of ideas for what they could do while Eleanor was at work.

One day he said, "Let's jump on the beds." They jumped on
Eleanor's bed first, then on Bucky's cot until the mattress went lumpy.
They couldn't jump on the bunk beds, so they jumped on the sofa instead.
It was fun for a while, but it made Teeny feel sick to her stomach. When
Eleanor got home, they got in trouble. She yelled and threatened them
with the belt. Usually she just sent them to bed early.

Hugh didn't live there. Leroy wasn't there either, and no one talked
about Doris anymore.

Bucky was in his last year of high school. He went to Baltimore
Polytechnic Institute, a public high school for smart boys who wanted to
be engineers. He got A's but didn't have friends or a girlfriend and didn't

do anything after school. At home he lay on his bed reading thick library books. There weren't many ways out for poor kids then. Joining the military was one of them. Bucky had already decided he would enlist after graduation. He worried he was too thin, but they took him anyway.

Maggie came to visit sometimes with her new husband, Eddie Greene. Maggie was proud of her diamond ring and introduced herself as Margaret Greene. Eddie was going to be a teacher. He was the only person in the family who had gone to college. Eleanor thought Maggie had done well.

The boys liked Eddie. Teeny did not. Eddie teased her in ways she didn't understand and paid attention to her for too long. She didn't know what was wrong, only that it made her feel tight and watchful. When Eddie was around, Maggie acted differently too, sharper somehow, and Teeny stayed close to Billy or found a reason to leave the room.

27 Muddy Shoes

Claire learned quickly what teachers liked.

She raised her hand to answer questions she knew the answer to, which was nearly all of them. Often her hand was already in the air before the teacher finished speaking.

The teacher would pause, look around the room, and say, "Anyone besides Claire want to answer the question?"

Teeny did not understand this. If she knew the answer, why wouldn't the teacher want it?

On her report card it said, Claire needs to learn that there are other children in the class.

Teeny thought that was unfair.

Even though school frustrated her, Teeny loved it. She liked being asked questions. She liked knowing the answers first. There were things about school she didn't understand, but that didn't stop her from wanting to do it right.

It had rained all night, and the school was still under construction, so there was mud everywhere. Claire wore her yellow raincoat and carried an umbrella as she walked up the grassy hill to the building. Her red Mary Janes—her ever-present corrective shoes—were splattered with mud by the time she got inside.

She wasn't the only one. Nearly all the children arrived with muddy shoes that day. One girl hadn't worn a raincoat or brought an umbrella. Her hair and clothes were soaked, and her shoes were covered in thick, heavy mud. The teacher told her to take them off and said the school had shoes she could wear, because hers were ruined.

Teeny went up to the teacher.

"My shoes are muddy too," she said. "Should I get a new pair?" The teacher said Claire's shoes could be cleaned and told her to get paper towels from the bathroom.

When Eleanor got home from work, Teeny told her about the shoes and the other girl. She asked why the school didn't want to give her new shoes too. Eleanor explained that the girl's shoes had already been in very bad condition, and that her parents didn't have money to buy her new ones. The school wanted to help.

Teeny thought about this for a long time.

She decided that she didn't fit in with the other children. She had evidence. She wasn't supposed to answer questions even when she knew the answer. Her shoes weren't the same as the others'. And she felt different; in a way she didn't know how to explain.

She didn't know how to say this to Eleanor, so she kept it inside.

28 Iron

Teeny swallowed the foul-tasting spoonful of liquid Eleanor held to her lips. It was thick and metallic, and it burned all the way down. "You're anemic," Eleanor said. "You have dark circles under your eyes. You need iron. So you have to take this." The same words came at dinner when a mound of gray-green canned spinach or a slab of fried beef liver landed on her plate. "You need to eat. You're skinny." Teeny stared at the food until it went cold. The liver smelled awful and had the texture of a pencil eraser. The spinach slid across her fork in a wet clump. She could not make herself swallow it.

Eleanor would coax at first. Then plead. Then her voice would sharpen. Sometimes there were threats. The rules did not change. Teeny still would not eat it. The battles happened over and over, like a song stuck on the same line.

At the parent-teacher conference, her teacher told Eleanor that Claire looked tired. She asked about the dark circles under her eyes. Eleanor promised to put her to bed earlier.
Teeny had already been going to bed at eight. After that meeting it became seven-thirty. The light would still be fading outside when she was told to go upstairs.

The teacher also said that Claire daydreamed. That she did not pay attention. Eleanor promised she would "have a talk with her."

Teeny did not feel tired at school. She was in first grade. She felt finished.

When there was a test, Claire's pencil moved quickly across the page. She was always the first one done. She stared out the window and waited while the other children pressed their erasers into the paper and chewed the ends of their pencils.

She did not know why it was like that. It simply was.

School was the place where her mind had to slow down and stand in line. While she waited, she slipped sideways into other worlds. Places where things made sense. Places where no one watched her plate or counted the shadows under her eyes.

At home, she slipped away too.

When Maggie and Eddie came to visit, the air in the house felt different. Eddie always found a way to be alone with her. In the hallway. In a bedroom. In the small space by the door. She shrank back when he came too close.

Her sister was in the kitchen. Water ran in the sink.

He called her over. He kept her there.

His hands would land on her where she did not want them.

She did not have words for what was happening. She did not have words that would have made it stop.

Billy was usually gone with his friends. Bucky had left for the Army. Eleanor worked long hours. Hugh was back, but he seemed farther away than when he had been gone.

Teeny learned to go very still.

It was easier that way.

29 Bike

Hugh, Eleanor, and Teeny were living in a tiny row house on an alley street in Baltimore and Claire was registered in another school. The place was more shack than house. The backyard was fenced, but it was nothing but packed dirt.

They had a dog now.

Hugh built Puddles a wooden doghouse with a rounded arch for a door. He said it was important to raise it off the ground so it would stay dry, and he attached wooden feet to the bottom. Teeny put an old blanket inside. Puddles had long silky hair, a long heavy body, a large head, and short legs. She was probably a Corgi, but no one really knew.

Hugh helped Teeny learn to ride a two-wheeler. He and Eleanor gave her a brand-new blue bicycle with long streamers hanging from the handlebars. At first it had training wheels. When Hugh decided she was steady enough, he took them off.

She was not allowed to go far.

The bicycle was kept in the basement. The basement door opened at ground level, under the front porch. The floor was dirt. It smelled damp and old.

Eleanor told Teeny she was not to go around the corner to Frederick Avenue. It was dangerous. She was also told to be careful which neighborhood children she played with. The children nearby were louder and rougher than she was. Sometimes she liked that.

One boy, bigger than she was, admired her bicycle. He was pushy. It seemed to come naturally to him.

"Let me ride it," he said.

"No."

"Just once."

"My mother won't let me lend it to anyone."

He spit between his teeth. "She won't know."

Teeny felt something tighten inside her. She was afraid he might hit her and take it anyway. But she did not move.

"Yes," she said. "She will know."

He sneered. "What, can she read your mind?"

Teeny looked straight at him.

"Yes," she said. "She can."

The boy hesitated. It was only a flicker, but she saw it. He kicked at the dirt and walked away.

Teeny stood beside her bicycle, holding the handlebars.

She had watched grown people lean toward Eleanor at the kitchen table, waiting for the turn of a card. She had seen the way her mother looked at someone and then said something that landed too close to the bone.

So when she said that Eleanor could read her mind, she meant it. And when Teeny held someone's gaze just a moment longer than necessary, they sometimes shifted, the way that boy had. She did not yet know that she was learning how.

30 Buses

Billy did not live in the little shack-house on the alley street with Hugh, Eleanor, and Teeny. He went back to his father's house—the house with the screaming baby and the poop on the floor.

Teeny could hear Eleanor upstairs crying for a long time after he left. The sound came down through the thin ceiling. Teeny sat still and listened. She did not know what to do with a grown woman's crying.

Aunt Addie and Hugh's other sister, Birdie, came to visit. They took a bus all the way from western Pennsylvania. They said they wanted to see Washington, D.C., and they wanted to take Teeny with them.

Addie was in a better mood than the last time Teeny had seen her. Still, there was something in her voice that made Teeny feel as if she were being measured and found lacking. Birdie was small and blonde and looked younger than she was. She wore shorts and diamond earrings and shoes with curled-up toes like something a genie might wear. Someone had called her a firecracker and she liked to prove it. She teased people to get a laugh. Sometimes she pinched Teeny just to watch her jump.

Teeny was used to riding buses. She had ridden them with Eleanor, and sometimes by herself, downtown to meet her after work. She was seven now, missing her two front teeth, and she knew how things worked. She knew to drop the coins into the metal box and tell the driver where she was going. She knew to sit as close to the driver as possible.

Eleanor had given her rules. Sit by yourself, close to the driver. If there was no empty seat, sit next to a white woman. If not, sit next to a Black woman. If there were no seats beside a woman, stand near the driver if he would let her. Hugh said everyone was equal and should sit wherever they pleased. Eleanor said the same. But some people did not agree, and it was better to be careful.

Teeny had never had trouble on a bus. She had never missed her stop. The drivers were kind to her. When she rode alone, she felt capable. Almost grown.

Addie and Birdie wanted to take a Greyhound bus to Washington. They called her Teeny, but with them she felt more like Claire. Watchful. Alert.

The bus to Washington was different from the city buses. It smelled like gasoline, vinyl seats, and something fried. The ride felt long. Addie and Birdie talked and laughed. Teeny watched the highway unspool through the window.

In Washington they walked and walked and walked. They were there all day and into the evening. They searched for monuments and asked for directions. By the time they found the White House, the gates were closed. The three of them gripped the iron bars of the fence. They slid their feet through as far as they could reach so they could say they had set foot on the White House lawn.

It was dark when they made their way back to the bus station. They caught the last bus to Baltimore. Eleanor was waiting when they got home.

Claire was too tired to explain anything.

31   Lice

Claire was entering another classroom. She had already attended five different schools.

When she was younger and did not have to go to school, moving felt almost natural. New rooms. New streets. A different view from the window. Now there were forms to fill out. Records to transfer. Teachers asking where she had come from. She counted the schools the way other children counted birthdays.

This school was large, with grades one through six. There were so many children that the hallways felt like rivers at dismissal. Claire was there for two days before she got bronchitis again.

They were living in a small apartment across the street from the school. It was bitterly cold. There was no heat. Eleanor tucked her into a wide bed with a cast-iron headboard and footboard. She rubbed Mustarole on Claire's chest. The sharp smell filled the room. She piled every blanket they owned on top of her.

Still, Teeny shivered.

Eleanor laid her winter coat over the blankets and tucked it in around her. "Now you're snug as a bug in a rug," she said. Teeny coughed and listened to the pipes knock in the walls. She was sick for a long time. By the time she was well enough to return to school, they had moved again.

She was registered as Claire Young in another school. Another building. Another classroom.

In this school they learned how the Pilgrims made butter. The teacher poured cream into a glass jar and passed it from desk to desk. Each child shook it until their arms ached. The cream thickened. The jar grew heavy. When it finally turned to butter, the teacher brought out Saltine crackers. Each student received one cracker with a small smear of the butter they had made together.

Claire had long, dark hair that fell past the middle of her back. It was thick and shiny. In the Thanksgiving play, she was chosen to be an Indian. That pleased her. Eleanor had told her that her great-grandmother on her mother's side was Iroquois. Eleanor said she had once seen beaded moccasins and clothing in a trunk when she was a girl.

Sometimes Eleanor braided Teeny's hair into two long plaits that lay over her shoulders.

One afternoon, Claire's scalp began to itch. She scratched it with the eraser of her pencil. When she pulled the pencil away, a small black bug clung to the rubber tip. Her stomach dropped. She tried to brush it off quietly, but Maxine, the girl behind her, leaned forward.

"You got lice," Maxine said matter-of-factly. She explained that lots of kids at this school had them.

"Black girls don't get lice," she added. "We put stuff on our hair. Only white people get lice."

Teeny felt the heat rise up her neck. She stared at her desk.

Maxine had told her other things, too. About how everybody was the same color when God made them, but he poured chocolate milk on the black people and white milk on the white people.

She wondered how anyone could think that. She didn't say anything. Like she didn't tell kids who still believed in Santa that Santa wasn't real.

The bell rang.

At home she burst into tears and told Eleanor about the bug in her hair. Eleanor's face tightened. She moved quickly. She wrapped a towel around Teeny's head and told her not to touch anything. "Stay right there," she said, and left for the store.

When she returned, she carried a box of medicated shampoo and a fine-toothed comb.

She bent Teeny over the kitchen sink and removed the towel carefully, as if something might leap out. The shampoo smelled sharp and chemical. Eleanor scrubbed and rinsed and scrubbed again.

Then she sat Teeny in a chair. Without much warning, she began cutting. Dark hair slid down the front of Teeny's dress and fell to the floor. Eleanor's mouth was set in a hard line. "I hope this works," she muttered. "Hugh's going to be mad your hair isn't long anymore." Teeny sat very still. She felt as if she had done something wrong.

When Eleanor finished, Claire's hair hung at her chin. As it dried, Eleanor parted it in small sections and pulled the fine-toothed comb through, wiping it on a paper towel each time.

"What's a nit?" Teeny asked quietly.

"Louse eggs," Eleanor said.

Teeny swallowed and tried not to gag.

Being small for her age was something people noticed.

One of her second-grade teachers dropped a pencil and looked around the room. "Claire, you're the smallest. Would you crawl under my desk and get it?" Claire slid out of her chair and under the desk. Dust clung to her knees. She handed the pencil back up. She didn't mind. It was more interesting than just sitting at her desk.

At this school, a girl in her grade stopped her most mornings near the milk line. The girl was bigger, already certain in her body. She stepped in front of Claire and held out her hand. "Give it." If Claire hesitated, the girl leaned closer. "I'll beat you up." Claire gave her the coins and drank water from the fountain instead. No one seemed to notice. Or if they did, nothing changed.

At home, Hugh beat her with a belt when he was angry. Eleanor sometimes used the belt, or punished her for making Hugh angry, or for waking him. Hugh was drunk, or passed out on the living room floor, or asleep and snoring loud enough to shake the air, or hung over and sharp. He went to work most days, but sometimes he was home when he wasn't expected. Teeny learned to listen before entering a room.

Sometimes Maggie came to take her to the apartment she shared with Eddie. Maggie was pregnant and wore maternity clothes that announced her condition. She smiled often. The smile seemed practiced. She was especially kind to Eleanor.

Eleanor treated those visits as relief. Teeny did not. They meant watching where Eddie stood and keeping a careful distance. They meant shrinking back when he came too close. They meant waiting for it to be time to go home.

Around this time, Teeny began twisting her hair around her finger. She did it without thinking. The strand wound tight, then loosened, then wound again. When Eleanor noticed, she told her to stop. "You'll ruin your hair."

Teeny put her hands down. Later, they rose again.

One afternoon at recess, Claire stood near the brick wall of the school, twisting her hair and watching the other children play dodgeball.

The ball struck hands and pavement with a steady rhythm. Children called to one another without looking.

Near her feet was a metal grate set into the ground. Someone had left a small empty glass juice bottle on top of it. She wore her red Mary Janes, thick-soled and sturdy. She looked at the bottle for a long moment. Then she drew her foot back and kicked. The bottle shattered. Glass skittered across the grate. Some pieces slipped through and disappeared. The sound was sharp enough that several children turned. A teacher crossed the playground toward her.

"Did you break that bottle?"

"Yes."

"Why?"

Claire looked at him. The other children had already gone back to their game.

She did not answer.

33   Maggie's House

Hugh was gone again. Maggie had suggested that Eleanor and Teeny move in with her, Eddie, and the baby. Their row house had enough room for everyone.

Maggie made no secret of her hope that Eleanor would get back together with her father, Ray. Eleanor had left him because he hit her, cheated on her, and talked to her like she was nothing. Since then, Eleanor had paired up with Hugh, and Ray had paired up with Gladys, who seemed to put up with everything. Maggie acted as if Gladys didn't exist. Eleanor made it clear she had no intention of going back to Ray, even if Hugh wasn't around.

Eleanor went to work, and Maggie watched Teeny after school. Claire adjusted to the new school quickly and made friends with a few girls. Just school friends. They didn't visit.

Maggie's house never felt like home. Eddie got close to Teeny in ways that made her freeze. He exposed himself and touched her. She didn't want to be touched.

When Eleanor wasn't around, Maggie could be sharp and cruel. Once, she scratched the back of Teeny's hand so deeply it left a scar.

Maggie would later say, "You deserved it. You were a terrible child."

Teeny moved through the house like a shadow, staying out of sight. Sometimes she pretended to be asleep. Eddie followed her everywhere. No corner was safe. No doorway private. Eleanor was at work. Maggie was nearby, talking on the phone or cleaning, always there, always close—but never looking.

Teeny counted the minutes, counting always against the clock on the wall. She never knew when he would appear, never knew what would happen next. She kept still. Always still.

Dread never left, even when it wasn't Eddie.

Eleanor did not beat Teeny as often as Hugh had, and not for the same reasons. Hugh drank and waited for something Teeny said to set him off. Eleanor did not drink. Sometimes she just went too far. She had a belt she liked. It was reversible, one color on each side, with a shiny buckle you could take off and snap back on. She used that.

Afterward, Eleanor told Teeny she would have to wear tights to school. It was already warm. The kind of day when the classroom windows were cracked open and the air felt heavy.

The tights were thick and hard to pull on. They stuck to her legs. In the schoolyard, standing in the sun, a girl kept looking down at Claire's legs. Claire said, "My mother thought it would be cold today and made me wear tights." The girl shook her head. "That's not true. You have welts on your legs. You're wearing tights to hide them."

Claire felt her face burn. She wished she could disappear or run away. She couldn't.

One evening, Maggie decided Eddie should take Teeny and the baby to a drive-in movie. Eleanor agreed.

The baby slept in the back. Teeny sat up front, eyes on the flickering screen. The speaker rattled from the window. Outside, the swings swung in the wind. Eddie's pants were open. He moved close. She crawled away from him, back toward the baby's seat. He reached for her. "I'll scream," she said. His face went red. She had never seen him look so angry. He zipped his pants and drove off before the movie ended.

Teeny couldn't remember what the movie had been.

She stopped twirling her hair. She started biting her fingernails.

Near the end of third grade, Eleanor and Claire moved with Hugh to a row house on Dryden Street in South Baltimore. Houses pressed shoulder to shoulder. Most had white marble steps; some were red brick, all scrubbed clean. Families sat on the stoops in the evenings. People knew who lived where.

Eleanor said she liked South Baltimore. She had lived there as a girl. Her mother, Annie Mae Murphy, came from the neighborhood before marrying John Deveraux and moving into a big house with a maid. After the divorce, Eleanor and her sister Letitia lived in South Baltimore with their mother. Their father's mother Minty decided Letitia was acceptable because she looked like John. Eleanor looked like Annie Mae. Not acceptable.

Eleanor said she had toured the VanCleve mansion once – toured, not visited. She had been cut out of the inheritance. She mentioned it often. "They had seven bathrooms," she said. "Family crest embedded in the floor of the entrance hall."

VanCleve was Minty's second husband. Eleanor said Minty had married up twice.

The house on Dryden Street was nothing like that. Floors slanted from front to back. The bathroom leaned more than the rest, built onto what had once been a porch. Cold in winter, hot in summer. Under it, a summer kitchen. No heat. Mostly storage.

Most other houses were neat and owner-occupied. The Youngs rented. The only other renters were a family everyone called the Hillbillies. Claire made friends next door. Janice was her age; Judy a year younger. Their mother and grandmother lived with them. Catholic school. "We're Catholic. You're a Public," they said. Claire let it go. Public sounded ignorant, but she wanted friends.

Judy was quick. Janice seemed slow. Judy liked the same games Claire liked. They roller skated in the street; metal clamps on their shoes sparking on the pavement. The girls had a club basement with knotty pine walls and a television built into the wall. Claire thought it was fancy. They usually played there. Claire knew not to invite them to play at her house.

One afternoon, the girls argued. Later no one remembered why. Janice swung her skates by the straps at Claire's head. Claire ducked. Something flipped inside her. She grabbed Janice by the hair, pulled her down, and pounded her head against the sidewalk. Judy screamed. Eleanor ran out, thinking Claire had been hurt. Claire sat on Janice, hitting her chest. Eleanor grabbed her under the arms and dragged her up the marble steps. Claire kicked as she was pulled away.

Inside, Eleanor asked what had happened. "She tried to kill me," Claire said.

In a few days it was over. They skated again. They played in the basement.

But Claire never trusted Janice after that.

35　Piano

When Claire was eight, she got a toy chord organ for Christmas. Many children had them that year. She wanted one too. Hers was the smallest model. The girls next door had a larger one with more buttons. Hers had three octaves, six chord buttons. That was enough. She played songs from the radio, picked them out by ear, testing each note until the melody sounded right.

One afternoon she called into the other room. "Listen to me play." Hugh and Eleanor came, standing behind her. Claire played the songs she had learned. When she finished, Hugh laughed. "Play that again." He stayed while she repeated it. Eleanor watched her hands, the way they curved over the keys, the way her wrist tilted slightly.

After that, Eleanor asked about piano lessons. There was no money. No piano. It did not matter.

Neighbor children went to Saint Brendan the Navigator. Nuns taught piano there. The church was three blocks away. Most families on the block were Catholic. Their children went to school there. Claire went to a public school two blocks past the church.

Eleanor asked the nuns if Claire could take lessons. They agreed. The price was low.

Claire liked touching the real piano. She did not like the lessons. The nun spoke flatly. Hands folded when not pointing at the music. Other children said the nun hit knuckles with a ruler. Claire watched for the ruler.

Eleanor looked for a piano. No money to buy one. She told her sister Letitia that Claire had talent. Letitia's neighbors had an upright piano from Germany, unused for years. They gave it to Claire.

It was a tall upright, built in the 1800s, carved with leaves across the front, a lighter color than the pianos at school or church. Hugh said it was solid oak. The bench opened. Inside, children's music books. Claire took out the easiest ones, practiced a few weeks. She did not return to the nun.

Eleanor arranged an audition at Peabody Preparatory. They could not afford the tuition. A large room. A grand piano. Steinway printed above the keys. Several adults sat close enough to see her hands. Eleanor said she played songs from the radio and had a few lessons.

One adult asked Claire to play anything. She sat straight; fingers curved as the nun had shown her. She played simple songs from one of the books she'd brought. The adults leaned forward, watching her hands. When she was finished one of them told her that she had good posture and beautiful fingering. Eleanor went into an office. Claire waited in the hallway. Polished wood floors, marble statues, quiet.

When Eleanor returned: "You start lessons next Saturday."

They took the bus home.

After Claire was accepted at Peabody, Eleanor spoke of education as something no longer theoretical—something Claire could reach and hold. Hugh agreed. Both believed their lives would have been broader if they had finished high school.

Hugh grew up in a rural place where high school required a train ride to the city. He was the second youngest of seven. The family could afford to send only the oldest boy.

Eleanor left school after eighth grade. Annie Mae was ill from an abortion she'd done herself. It was illegal. There was a baby in the house. Letitia refused to stay home. Eleanor did. She fed the baby. She tended her mother. She put her books away. She remained until Ray Parks entered her life. Later, she left him. With Hugh, life was hard in other ways, but they shared this: school mattered.

So, when Claire's teacher said the school had been given season tickets for four students and one parent each to the Baltimore Symphony Orchestra Youth Concert Program, and Claire's name was on the list, Eleanor did not hesitate.

They went to the Lyric Theater. The hall filled with children and parents. The orchestra played a piece. Then the conductor turned to the audience and explained it—how a theme returned, why the strings fell quiet before the brass entered. Claire sat upright in her seat and watched his hands. She knew why she had been chosen.

Eleanor stood close to a uniformed guard at City Hall and spoke in a lowered voice. Claire waited close by. On days when school was closed, Eleanor took her through public buildings and places of interest. The building was open to the public, but not all of it. There was no tour that day.

Eleanor pointed toward Claire. The guard glanced over at her, then back at Eleanor. He smiled. Eleanor crooked her finger. "Teeny. Come here." The guard chose a key from his ring and opened a side door. "The inner sanctum," he said, pleased with himself.

It was an exploration day. Eleanor moved through the city as if it belonged to her. She had lived in Baltimore most of her life. She knew which corridors held murals, which staircases ended in balconies, which doors might open if she asked in the right tone.

They stepped into the mayor's outer office. School was closed. City employees were off. The room was still. Mahogany furniture. Heavy drapes. A broad desk where a secretary usually sat. Chairs set in a row for waiting. The building had been raised in the Gilded Age, when cities proved themselves with stone and ornament. Eleanor's eyes settled on the interior door behind the secretary's desk. The guard followed her gaze. Another key. Another lock.

Inside, the mayor's office was larger. A massive desk. Uneven stacks of paper left in place. A glass-front cabinet with historical objects arranged for display. The guard stood straighter here. "Want to see a secret?" he asked. "Yes," Eleanor said. "Yes," Claire echoed. He pressed on a seam in the wood paneling. A narrow door released. Behind it, a short passage and a stairwell.

"This is where he goes if he doesn't want to see someone." They laughed. The panel closed. The wall returned to itself.

37　Twilight Zone

Every Friday Claire took the bus downtown by herself and met Eleanor at the sewing factory at five o'clock, when the women came filing out. If the bus ran early, Claire walked up to the second floor of the old brick building and waited in the factory office. She sat quietly until the bell rang. The secretaries and the owner, Mr. Eli, were polite but mostly ignored her. Some of the women knew her. A few had even come to the house to visit Eleanor and have their cards read. When they saw Claire waiting, they would smile and say, "Hi, Teeny."

Eleanor was always in a good mood on Fridays. Sometimes they went to the White Coffee Pot diner near the factory and ordered crab cake platters to go. Other times they took the bus home and stopped at George's for a hot dog and a chocolate milkshake. The sign said "George's Lunch," though they stayed open later than lunch.

They carried the food home and ate in front of the television. They watched *The Twilight Zone*. Hugh was never there. He went from work straight to the neighborhood bar and didn't come home until after Claire was in bed.

Claire and Eleanor both liked *The Twilight Zone*. The stories were strange and ended with a twist. The twinkling theme music meant something unusual was about to happen.

One Friday, while they watched television, Eleanor brushed Claire's long hair. She complained about the tangles and pulled harder than usual. Claire said it hurt. Eleanor kept brushing and said, almost to herself, "All men are rats." She said it often.

She stopped brushing.

"Teen, call the bar and ask if Hugh is there."

Claire called. In her small voice she said, "Is my daddy there? Hugh. He usually sits on the stool near the door." The bartender knew him. "I'm sorry, hon. He's not here." Claire told Eleanor what he said. Eleanor answered, "One lies and the other swears to it."

There was a knock at the door. It was Uncle Leroy. Eleanor let him in and came back to sit behind Claire with the hairbrush. Claire stayed on the floor. Uncle Leroy stood across the room, looking uneasy. "He sent me by with this," he said, holding out some money.

Eleanor lifted the brush and shook it at him from where she sat. She said a few sharp words. Leroy stepped backward, hands raised. "Don't kill the messenger," he said, with a thin laugh.

Claire did not know exactly what was happening, but she knew Hugh was in trouble.

38   Salvation Army

Eleanor found things for Claire to do after school. Claire wore a key to the back door on a string around her neck, she could let herself in and watch television until Eleanor came home. Eleanor did not want her outside. She did not want her letting anyone into the house. Sitting alone in front of the television was not enough for Claire.

There was an after-school program at the recreation center where children made ashtrays out of clay and braided lanyards out of plastic cord. Eleanor signed her up. She also enrolled her in the Sunbeams, run by the Salvation Army. It was like Brownies, but not. Claire worked through the book and earned every badge.

The Salvation Army was on Light Street, across from the rec center in South Baltimore. Eleanor trusted them. They had run the nursery school Claire attended.

It did not seem like Eleanor's style. The women wore uniforms. The men wore uniforms. The brass instruments were polished and loud. The congregation clapped in rhythm. Claire thought it was strange and felt her face get hot and her stomach clench when people clapped or sang with their eyes closed. On Sundays she went there with Eleanor while most of the neighborhood went to Saint Brendan the Navigator. She did not mention it at school. She did not mention it on Dryden Street.

Hugh did not go with them to the Salvation Army church. He didn't much like most churches. He always said that he respected Quakers but didn't go to their church either. He especially didn't like proselytizing. When Jehovah's Witnesses came to the door with Watchtower magazines he called them "God damned Russelites" and said the religion had started with a man named Russell in Pittsburgh. He called their Catholic neighbors "Papists." He had a name for everything. Claire liked the names. She liked knowing why.

She learned to play the cornet at the Salvation Army. She stood in a row with other children and held it the way they showed her. That December she had a part in the Christmas pageant. People applauded and she felt like she did a good job.

In the summer she went to Camp Tomahawk in West Virginia for a week. It was also run by the Salvation Army. Hugh and Eleanor dropped her off with a duffel bag. She had packed according to the list and checked each item with a pencil. The bunkhouse was rounded and made of corrugated metal. Inside were rows of metal bunk beds. The air smelled like damp canvas and soap.

There was always something scheduled. Crafts. Songs. Swimming in a creek instead of a pool. The counselors led them into the water. Claire did not like the feel of rocks shifting under her feet or the brush of fish against her legs. Turtles surfaced and disappeared. The water moved on its own. She went in anyway.

She did well at most things. She made friends for the week. They did not write afterward.

Salvation Army meetings, practices, and camp sat apart from the rest of her life. She did not tell her school friends. She did not tell the girls on her block. It was not something she mixed in with the rest of her life.

39 Charisma

Eleanor told Claire she had registered her for ballet lessons at the rec center. "Ballet will make you more graceful."

Eleanor was always telling Claire to stand up straight. Other people said she had good posture. Eleanor called her awkward and clumsy.

Once Maggie said Claire did not have a "good" walk. Claire did not know what that meant. It seemed to have something to do with the way men looked at you. Claire already wished Maggie's husband, Eddie, would not look at her at all.

Eleanor took Claire shopping for ballet clothes. They bought a black leotard and pink tights. They went to a special store downtown for ballet slippers. Claire got a shiny black case with pink ballet shoes printed on it to carry her things. Eleanor talked about the class the whole way home. She said when Claire got further along, she would make her a tutu.

The teacher wore a skirt over her leotard and tights and carried a long stick. A woman sat at the piano and played while the girls moved. Mirrors covered one wall. A wooden rail ran along it. It was called a barre. There were about twelve girls in the class. They learned the five positions. They bent their knees in plié and rose up in relevé. Some girls were eager and smiled at themselves in the mirrors. Claire stood where she was told and did what she was told. She liked it well enough. She did not think she wanted to be a ballerina.

One girl named Suzie was very round. Her leotard was blue instead of black. Claire watched her struggle to pull herself up at the barre. No one said anything about it. Claire felt sorry for her.

The rec center held parties and recitals. At Halloween there was a costume party. Eleanor did not believe in store-bought costumes. She put one together from things at home. "You'll be a gypsy," she said. Claire wore a long full skirt with a wide scarf tied around her hips. A smaller scarf covered the top of her head. Her bangs showed in the front, and her long hair fell out from under it in the back. She stacked bracelets up both arms and wore her ballet slippers. She liked the way the skirt moved when she turned.

On the way to the party, Eleanor talked about the teachers and the

older girls. One of them, Kate, helped with classes. She had blonde
hair and blue eyes and smiled when she spoke. "That girl Kate has charisma,"
Eleanor said. Claire asked what charisma meant. Eleanor said it was an
extra spark. It made people notice you. It made them like you. "Do I have
that spark?" Claire asked.

Eleanor looked down at her as they walked.

"No."

They kept walking.

At the party Claire saw friends and her favorite teacher. She played
games. She drank soda and ate candy.

Later she and Eleanor walked home. Eleanor talked. Claire did not
say much. Eleanor did not notice.

40   Grandparents

Annie Mae dragged one leg. Her right arm hung still at her side and did not work.

Eleanor said that years ago, when Annie Mae was a younger woman, she had been standing at a bus stop. A man started talking to her and tried to get her to go with him. He was holding a bottle and drinking from it. Annie Mae said no. She turned her back so he would know she did not want to talk. The man hit her in the head with the bottle. He left her on the street. After that, she couldn't walk right.

Annie Mae lived alone in an efficiency apartment on Carey Street in Southwest Baltimore. The room was small and dusty. The stove, the table, the bed, and a wooden rocking chair were all in the same space. Annie Mae sat in the rocking chair by the window most of the day. A large paper bag of candy rested on the floor beside her chair.

Sometimes when Eleanor and Claire were out shopping, Eleanor bought Annie Mae a housedress. It had to have a pocket on the left side so she could reach it with her good hand. Most dresses had the pocket on the right. Her favorite color was pink.

Annie Mae had trouble opening cans and buttoning things. She lived alone anyway. Eleanor tried to find small ways to make things easier for her, but there were not many household items made for people who could only use one hand, and there was no money for special equipment.

When they visited, Annie Mae held out the candy bag with her good hand. "Teeny, would you like a piece of candy?" There were peppermints, caramels, hard butterscotch, and pieces wrapped in wax paper with the ends twisted tight. Sometimes Claire chose one. There was nothing else to do in the apartment. The visits were short.

At home later, Eleanor told stories about her own childhood. After her parents divorced, Annie Mae drank. There was no telephone. Eleanor said she went from bar to bar looking for her mother. She was the middle child. Her older sister, Letitia, was rarely home. By twelve, Eleanor was carrying her baby brother on her hip while she searched.

Once, she stood in the doorway of a bar and saw Annie Mae dancing on a table, holding up her skirt while men clapped. Eleanor's face changed when she told that story. Claire watched her and did not say anything. She was glad her mother did not drink.

Other children talked about their grandmothers. Claire didn't talk about Annie Mae. She didn't talk about Hugh's mother either. She had never met her.

She did not talk about grandfathers. Eleanor's father had died before Claire was born. Irish, Hugh's father, died when Claire was a baby. People told stories about Irish, but Claire did not know him.

On television, grandparents sat at kitchen tables and gave advice. Her friends' grandparents made them food and brought presents on birthdays and at Christmas. Claire knew about grandparents, but only from the outside.

41 Sparky

Eleanor, Hugh, and Claire were walking past the bar when they saw a small group of men gathered on the corner. Uncle Leroy stood in the middle of them. At his feet was a small black-and-white Boston terrier. The dog waited while Leroy gave a quiet command. It sat. It rolled over. It stood up on its hind legs. The men clapped and laughed.

Claire asked if it was his dog.

"I'm watching him for a friend," Leroy said. "Just a few days. His name is Sparky."

He held out his arms. Sparky jumped through them. The dog moved fast and then froze, waiting for the next word. Claire thought he looked like a circus dog. The men were still laughing when Sparky lifted his leg and peed on Hugh's pant leg.

Everyone looked down at the same time.

The men howled. "Guess he knows who he likes," someone said.

Claire held her breath.

Eleanor laughed harder than anyone. Hugh's face changed once, then again. Then he started laughing too.

"That little son of a bitch has a lot of nerve," he said.

Eleanor wiped her eyes and steered them back toward the house so Hugh could change his pants.

Later they returned to the bar for dinner. Sparky was gone. The corner was quiet again. After they ate, they walked home. The streetlamps flickered on.

Eleanor and Hugh sat on the front steps. Claire played tag with the girls next door under the streetlamp at the corner. She was not allowed past where Eleanor could see her.

Most evenings she could stay out until the lights came on. Eight or ten kids gathered in the alley. They ran races. They played hide-and-seek and tag. Claire was usually the fastest. When they played Mother May I, she asked for umbrella steps or giant steps. Regular steps felt plain.

When Eleanor called out, she answered right away and ran back toward the house.

42 Smoke

Everyone said Eleanor was a bad cook. Eleanor said it herself. She laughed when she said it. She liked food plain. Meat cooked through—fried, boiled, or baked until there was no pink left. A peanut butter sandwich was smooth peanut butter spread on a slice of white bread and folded once. No jelly. No chunks. Meat loaf was ground beef, chopped onion, salt. Nothing else.

Everyone agreed Eleanor could cook one thing well: mashed potatoes. She peeled them at the kitchen table. Boiled them until they broke under a fork. She drained the pot, tipping it toward the sink, lid loose, steam on her face. A slab of margarine. A splash of milk. A pinch of salt—thrown over her left shoulder if any spilled, to keep the devil away. Metal against metal, she mashed them in the same pot. Mashed potatoes most nights.

Hugh often cooked for himself. He used his Bowie knife instead of the kitchen knives Eleanor used. A baked bean sandwich. Thick slices of Limburger that cleared the kitchen. Once he ate something dark and knotted. He said it was squirrel. Claire put a piece in her mouth and spat it into the trash. He ate sardines from a tin, the lid bent back. When Claire said "eww" and held her nose, he laughed.

When she was small, there was no choice. A plate in front of her. She had to finish it. She and Eleanor fought over food. Eleanor told people, "She's a picky eater." By nine, Claire cooked for herself. A can of soup. A frozen dinner slid into the oven. A grilled cheese browned in a pan. Later she cooked from scratch—pepper, onions, garlic, dried herbs. She tasted as she went. Eleanor took a bite and pushed the plate away. "You shitted it all up," she said, and would not eat it.

Cooking did not always go well in the house. The house often smelled like something burned. Hugh fell asleep with lit cigarettes. Most of the time Eleanor caught it. A scorched cushion would end up in the sink, then in the backyard, splashed with a bucket of water and left against the fence.

One night the smoke woke Claire. So did the yelling. She stood in her doorway and looked across the hall. Eleanor and Hugh were dragging a smoking mattress toward the front window. They heaved it up and pushed it out. It hit the sidewalk below with a flat thud.

Claire started to speak. Eleanor saw her. "Go back to bed."

Claire went. A little later Eleanor walked through the house opening windows. A fan hummed in the hallway. Claire kept her eyes closed.

Another time there was no one home but Hugh. School was closed. Eleanor was at work. Claire was next door in Janice and Judy's basement clubroom. Their grandmother made them bologna sandwiches and cut them in halves. They were playing Monopoly when they smelled smoke. They decided Claire should check.

When she opened her front door, smoke rolled out toward her. It smelled worse than anything she had ever smelled. Hugh was stretched out on the living room floor, snoring.

In the kitchen a small enamel pan sat on the stove. The flame was high. Inside the pan were two eggs burned black in their shells.

Claire turned off the gas. She opened the windows. She shook Hugh's shoulder and yelled his name. He staggered into the kitchen, picked up the pan with a dish towel, and ran water into it. It hissed and spit. He dropped the whole thing into the trash.

There was some cursing. No talking.

Claire stood in the kitchen. She looked at him. "I've got it," he said. "Go back to whatever you were doing."

By the time Eleanor came home, Hugh was gone. Claire told her what happened. Eleanor stood still for a moment, then muttered, "Asshole," and began setting the house back in order. That night Claire and Eleanor ate TV dinners on folding trays in front of the television. They did not talk about Hugh.

43   Queequeg

When they lived on Dryden Street, Claire felt like she belonged to something.

Nell's Store was across the street. Claire went there to buy cigarettes for her parents and penny candy for herself with the change. Buford's was in the basement of the corner house. Eleanor sent her there for lunch meat—a quarter pound of chipped ham, a quarter pound of American cheese, half a loaf of white bread. Sometimes it was Taylor's ham. Sometimes canned corned beef. There was a pharmacy up the hill with a soda fountain. Claire could sit at the long marble counter and order a Coke with a straw. If she had enough money, an ice cream soda.

The Cas Bar was across Fort Avenue. It belonged to a man named Casimir. Everyone called him Cas. That was Hugh's place. Riverside Park was a couple of blocks away. There was a pool in the summer. Claire played outside with the other children. She was where she was supposed to be.

Some things were different. The other children were not reading *Moby-Dick* or *Atlas Shrugged* in fourth grade. Their mothers did not read cards for people at the kitchen table. Their fathers did not leave the car in the middle of the street overnight because they were too drunk to park it.

Claire liked *Moby-Dick*. Queequeg was her favorite. She liked the way he threw the bones to tell the future. She liked his tattoos. She liked that he didn't look like anyone else on the ship. She read *Atlas Shrugged* because Bucky had read it and she liked the title. He came home on leave from the Army with different books from the ones on Eleanor and Hugh's shelves. She asked to borrow it. He said yes, but only if she promised to look up every word she did not know. She kept a dictionary beside her and kept her promise.

Bucky was in the Army's Special Forces. He wore a green beret and a braided cord over his shoulder. There was a pin on his uniform shaped like a parachute with wings. He told her he worked in Intelligence and could speak five languages fluently.

Bucky and Hugh did not like each other. They were both quiet. They both read. They stayed out of each other's way.

Bucky did not talk much, but he answered Claire's questions when she asked them. He was kind to her. Sometimes he seemed far away, as if he were listening to something she could not hear.

Hugh ignored Claire unless she amused him or annoyed him. When he laughed, she liked him. She could not always tell which it would be.

Hugh's closest friend was his brother Leroy. Bucky's closest friend was Maggie's husband, Eddie. They read the same books and talked for hours. Claire wondered if Bucky knew what Eddie was doing to her. She decided he did not. Eddie was careful. Bucky was not cruel. He was safe.

Two hundred twenty-six, two hundred twenty-seven. Claire counted the marble stairs in her head as she climbed the spiral. The steps curved tightly against the stone. Her hand slid along the cool rail. Elizabeth's shoes tapped behind her. They did this every week in the hour between piano and theory.

Nine revolutions. Claire liked knowing the number. She liked the turn and turn again, the faint light coming in from above, the air thinning near the top. When they reached the top level of the Washington Monument, the city opened in four directions.

Row houses laid out in brick lines. Church steeples. The harbor. She found the prison yard without meaning to. Small figures moved inside a square of fence. Back and forth. She watched them circle. From above, everything fit inside its borders.

Elizabeth lived on Dryden Street, too. Her mother worked as a secretary downtown. Her father read meters for Baltimore Gas and Electric. They did not spend much time together in the neighborhood, but every Saturday they went together to the Peabody Preparatory department for their lessons.

"That was lovely, Claire. You've been keeping up with your practice." Miss Valentine spoke quietly. She set the metronome ticking and placed it closer to the keyboard. Each week she put a new piece on the stand, slightly more difficult than the last. Claire liked the building—the tall ceilings, the wide staircases that curved in a long sweep, the echo that followed footsteps down the hall. The rooms felt measured. They opened around her. She walked slower and more carefully there.

There were report cards at Peabody, the same as at school. Elizabeth said she had to take a test at the end of the semester. Claire asked Miss Valentine about hers. "You don't need to take a test."

Miss Valentine said her weekly work was enough. When the report card came, there was an A, right where it belonged. Claire looked at it for a long time. She folded it along its crease and put it back in the envelope.

After lessons the girls met in the lunchroom. Mostly adults sat at small tables, leaning toward one another, hands moving as they talked.

Instrument cases rested on the floor beside their chairs. There were vending machines along one wall. One held sandwiches. When you pressed a button, a metal coil turned and the sandwich slid forward, stopping behind a square of glass. You lifted the plastic door and took it out. Claire watched the mechanism catch and release.

Sometimes they ate there. More often they went outside to Mount Vernon Square.

The square was divided into four sections, each facing a different direction, each a block long. There were fountains. In one circular pond stood a bronze boy balanced on a turtle's back, one leg raised, arms lifted. Water came up in a circular spray around him, from bronze cattails.

Claire sat on the cement edge and trailed her fingers in the water. Elizabeth wandered toward a bed of flowers across the square.

A voice sounded behind her.

She turned. A man stood too close. His beard was thin and uneven. His coat hung past his knees though the day was warm. Dirt darkened the cuffs. He asked how old she was.

"Ten," Claire said.

He laughed. The sound was low. He said something about the changes that were coming to her body, then drifted away across the path.

Claire wiped her wet hand on her skirt. She found Elizabeth near the flowers. "Let's go back," she said.

They crossed the square and went inside, the conservatory doors closing firmly behind them.

45   Barbie

Eleanor had always encouraged Claire to make things. She brought home craft kits, workbooks, and paint-by-number sets. Eleanor and Hugh worked on the paint-by-numbers too. The finished pictures hung in the kitchen and hallway.

Claire made clothes for her dolls. She did not use patterns. She cut and folded and pinned until something fit. She liked deciding how the skirts would flare or where a sleeve should gather.

She wanted a Barbie doll. The commercials called Barbie a "Teenage Fashion Model." She wore fitted dresses and high heels. Eleanor did not like the look of her at first. Claire saved her allowance and bought one herself at a store on Light Street.

Even Eleanor came around. She used scraps from the factory and made small dresses and coats for the doll. Claire's Barbie, her records, and the piano were her favorite things.

The girls in the neighborhood all had Barbies. They sat on marble steps and made up long stories about apartments and jobs and boyfriends. Claire preferred making the clothes. It made her want to sew for herself.

The treadle sewing machine in the bedroom was older than anyone in the house. Eleanor said it was an antique. It was black cast iron with a gold pattern worn thin from hands. The silver bobbin was smooth and heavy in Claire's palm.

It did not hum like other machines. You had to start it by turning the wheel and then pump the treadle with your feet. The rhythm mattered. Too slow and it stalled. Too fast and the stitches ran.

Eleanor pinned a paper pattern to the fabric and showed Claire how to cut along the thin lines. Claire leaned forward, guiding the cloth through the needle, her feet working the treadle below. The dress came together piece by piece.

Eleanor watched. "I think you might be better than me at this," she said.

Claire wore the dress to school the next day. When girls asked where she got it, she said, "I made it."

She liked the way that sounded.

46 Ring of Fire

Hugh, Eleanor, and Claire entered O'Henry's through the side door marked Dining Room. Claire was no longer allowed in the front room of a bar. Eleanor said she was too big for that now.

She could still play the jukebox. She fed coins into the slot and pressed the buttons carefully. Tennessee Ernie Ford sang "Sixteen Tons." She chose it because her parents liked it. She played Johnny Cash singing "Ring of Fire" because everyone liked that one. It was her favorite.

Around that same time, Hugh said, "Don't call me Daddy in front of people. Call me Hugh." Claire asked why. "He doesn't want people to think he's old," Eleanor said. Hugh laughed. Eleanor laughed with him.

They had been living on Dryden Street longer than Claire had ever lived anywhere. Some faces at Clement School looked familiar. From third grade, when she had first arrived. Recognition had never happened before. She had always been the new kid.

Eleanor declared the large front room the playroom. The piano stood against one wall. Games, coloring books, and dolls were stacked nearby. Hugh and Leroy brought home a small record player that only played 45s and a box of records that had once been in a jukebox. The player had a tall spindle that held a stack. Claire would load ten records at a time and let them drop and play one after another. She knew every word to every song in the box.

Hugh and Leroy often brought gifts. Jewelry for Eleanor. Once, a fur coat. For Claire, there were educational toys—a microscope in a wooden case with glass slides, a telescope she carried to Federal Hill Park with Billy to look at the harbor and the sky.

Eleanor said the men shopped at the "hock shop." Claire asked what that was. Eleanor explained that people took things there when they needed money. If they paid it back, they got their things again. If not, the store kept them and sold them. Claire felt sorry for the people who did not come back.

Sometimes Billy stayed with them on Dryden Street. Sometimes he stayed with his father. He was older now and popular. Girls grew soft and fluttery around him. They giggled, tipped their heads, and blinked their eyes more than usual. Some asked Claire when he would be home again. He still spent time with her, but less often. He had other places to be. Eleanor had names for each of her children. Billy was "the Cute One." Maggie was "the Pretty One." Bucky was "the Smart One." Claire was "the Baby."

In fourth grade, the entire school took IQ tests. The results were not given to the students, only to their parents. At the parent-teacher conference, the teacher told Eleanor that Claire had scored higher than anyone in the school. Eleanor did not tell her.

Later, the teacher told the class that someone in the room had earned the highest score in the whole building. She would not say who. The children began guessing. Most decided it must be Carl, a small boy with red hair who always got good grades.

No one guessed Claire.

Claire did not guess herself.

47   Broken Doll

Fluoroscopes and X-rays were ordinary for Claire. Doctors listened to her chest. There was always something there—congestion, a shadow, a question. She had dark circles under her eyes and pale skin This was routine. Eleanor would look at her and say she looked sickly.

Eleanor commented on everything. She would sigh and say, "You'll have to start wearing makeup young," though she wore little herself besides lipstick. She studied Claire the way other mothers studied report cards. A high forehead, better with bangs. Pale skin, fixable later with powder. Straight hair, that could be curled. She called her "little and skinny." Claire could not tell what belonged to illness and what was simply wrong with her.

In fourth grade she was sick again, the fever climbing and not coming down. The classroom tilted. The nurse called Eleanor at work, and Eleanor arrived and took her to the hospital in a taxi. The doctor said it was scarlet fever. There was medicine, but it did not seem to work.

The prescription was expensive, and Eleanor and Hugh borrowed money for it. Claire had always been told to say she was allergic to penicillin because it made her turn blue and stop breathing. This medicine was different. She reacted anyway, and things thinned out and blurred.

She was back at the hospital, half-awake on an examination table. The doctor told Eleanor that she could get worse. There could be heart damage. Nerve damage. She could die. Claire heard him. She thought, *He's wrong. I'm not going to die.* She felt very sick. Her skin peeled in sheets. The skin underneath was red and tender. She was sick for a long time.

Eleanor went to work. Hugh was not expected to manage sick children. He was either gone or asleep in a chair. Eddie said he would check on her. He did what he always did. She was too weak to speak much. Things happened around her.

Before the fever, her class had been learning to square dance. They were to be dancing dolls under a Christmas tree in the pageant. She did not know the steps and was slow to learn them, but she liked rehearsing with the others. She liked having a place among them.

By the time she returned to school there was one rehearsal left.

Eleanor bought her a green print skirt that flared when she turned. Her hair was braided. A neckerchief was tied at her throat. Even Eleanor said she looked cute.

On stage, when it was her turn, Claire started the dance but couldn't follow the steps. Everyone moved around her, doing do-si-do and allemande left. The music went on. The other children continued to dance. She stood still in the middle while they moved around her. When the dance ended, the audience laughed and clapped hard.

Afterward, people told her how cute it was.

They were supposed to be dancing dolls. She had not danced. In her mind that made her the broken one. She did not understand what was cute about that.

48 Perspective

Hugh liked history. Eleanor liked museums and anything that felt polished
and important. They went to historical sites. They went to museums.
If admission was free or cheap, they went. Claire went with them.

They went to Fort McHenry. The brick walls were thick. The flag
snapped in the wind. Cannons faced the water. They went to Gettysburg.
The fields were wide and open. There were fences and monuments and
rows of cannons. They walked the decks of the *Constellation* in the harbor.
The wood was dark and worn smooth. The ropes were coiled neatly. They
went to the Flag House, with its narrow rooms and steep stairs.
There were many exhibits about war.

Claire looked at the buildings. She looked at the windows and doors
and tried to imagine the rooms lit by candles. She was not interested in war.

They went to old houses. At the Carroll Mansion Eleanor said her
ancestors had lived there. The ceilings were high. The floors creaked. They
went to Edgar Allan Poe's house. The rooms were small and plain. They
went to see his grave. There were two monuments for him. One where he
was buried in the back of the cemetery and another big marble monument
near the front gate. Claire liked his stories. She liked that he had lived in
the same city she lived in.

On drives in the country, they looked for abandoned houses. If they
saw one, they slowed down. One time Hugh pulled over. They got out
and walked down a dirt road. The weeds were tall. The air was hot. It was
summer. Grasshoppers were everywhere. They jumped from the weeds.
They hit Claire's legs. They flew at her face. Eleanor and Hugh brushed
them away and kept walking. They were taller. Claire could not see the
house through the trees. She could see the grasshoppers. She screamed and
could not stop. They went back to the car. No one said anything. Claire
knew they were angry.

Eleanor took Claire to the main branch of the Pratt Library. The
building was stone, cool even in summer. The floors shone. Voices echoed.
There were listening rooms with headphones where Claire could sit alone
and play records. She had her own library card. She chose her own books.
On other days they went to the museums.

The museums were her favorite. They went to the Walters. The rooms were quiet and dim. There were glass cases and mummies wrapped in linen. They went to the Peale Museum. Portraits covered the walls. Eleanor said some of the faces were ancestors.

The Baltimore Museum of Art was Claire's favorite. Two stone lions sat outside. Wide steps led up to the doors. The bronze Thinker sat heavy and still. Each time she saw them, she felt a little thrill, ready for whatever fun waited inside.

Claire walked through the bright rooms. She loved the ancient mosaics. Tiny pieces of stone forming pictures on ancient floors. She was drawn to the modern and contemporary art. The colors were vibrant, saturated, deliberate. The sculptures were large scale, smooth and flowing.

These new works were not portraits of generals or rooms preserved behind velvet ropes. They were decisions made in the present tense. Claire had been making decisions too. Cut paper. Repeated images. Bright color. Words lifted from somewhere else and set down again.

She saw it as art. Art was not a distant inheritance. It was a practice. It was something a person could do daily and call work. The idea settled without announcement.

A person could be an artist.

49 Allowance

There were times when Eddie persuaded Eleanor that he should be in the house with Claire when no other adults were there.

One morning, Eddie was there after everyone had gone except for Claire. She was in the kitchen making her own breakfast. Eddie followed her around the kitchen table, as he unzipped his pants and exposed himself. He was laughing. Claire kept moving to stay out of reach. In circling the table, she knocked over the sugar bowl. Sugar spread across the tabletop and onto the floor. He stopped and looked at the mess. He laughed and told her she was going to get in trouble for that. Later, she did get in trouble—for not cleaning up the sugar. That order of events fixed itself in her mind.

Another time that year, when she was almost eleven, she was home from school with a fever. By then, these visits had been happening for years. There was one detail that was always the same. He carried a large jar of Vaseline. He kept it in the glove compartment of his car and brought it inside with him. The jar appeared each time. Before Claire had language for what he was doing, she understood what the jar meant. For years afterward, the sight of Vaseline made her stomach turn.

Eddie offered to stop by and check on her while she was sick. Her mother agreed. He sat on the sofa and exposed himself again. He opened the jar. Claire stood up and moved away from him, though she felt weak. He asked how much allowance she received each week. When she told him, he said he would give her twice that amount if she did what he wanted. She said no.

He said he would not touch her. He said he loved her.

"I love you more than I love your sister."

Something in her mind caught on that.

Not right.

As if she would want that.

She said no again.

For the first time during one of these visits, she walked out of the house. She did not explain. She did not ask permission. She left him there.

Outside, she stood on the sidewalk. She wondered if she would get in trouble for leaving the house while she was sick, or for leaving it unattended if he chose to go. She did not know what the right action was. She only knew she could not stay.

She did not yet know what would follow. She only knew that she had stepped out of the room. Later, she would remember that she could do that.

50   One Eye Open

The stores downtown stayed open late on Thursday nights. Claire met
Eleanor after work and they went shopping.

Eleanor knew about clothes. In the department stores she picked up
a dress and said, "Feel this." She turned a sleeve inside out. "Look at the
stitching." She checked the tags for brand names. In the discount stores
they stood over long tables and moved through the piles. Eleanor rubbed
the fabric between her fingers. She held things up to the light. Sometimes
she nodded. She could sew. She could change buttons. She could take in
a seam or let one out. She said it was the details that mattered. She told
Claire that clothes made a difference. She showed her what to look for,
one garment at a time.

Even the discount stores cost more than Eleanor usually had. Many
of them offered lay-a-way. Eleanor put a dollar down and paid a dollar
a week until the balance was gone. That night they were picking up
the dress. Claire loved it. The skirt had layers of semi-sheer fabric and a
sewn-in crinoline. The bodice had small tucks down the front. The sleeves
puffed and then narrowed into tight cuffs.

When they got home, Hugh was asleep on the couch. One eye was
partly open. This was not unusual.

He had been in a car accident years earlier. A thin scar ran across
his forehead. As he got older, the lines showed on one side more than the
other. His left eye did not always close all the way when he slept.

Claire once asked about the accident. It had happened before she
was born. Hugh had received a draft notice. The night before he was to
leave, he and Leroy and some friends had been out drinking. They drove
too fast. The car hit a tree. Hugh went through the windshield.

He said he lay on the hood and could hear but could not move.
A policeman said, "This one's dead." Head wounds bleed heavily. He lived.
The nerves in his forehead were damaged. The military changed its mind.
Hugh slept on the couch while Eleanor and Claire carried the box
upstairs. They set it on the bed and untied the string. The tissue paper
made a soft sound when they folded it back.

Claire felt her breath catch. Eleanor lifted the dress and hung it in the closet.

Claire waited for a place to wear it.

During scarlet fever her skin peeled away in sheets. By September she had grown six inches. Her dresses ended above the knee. Eleanor let down the hems.

She was eleven.

At Clement School she was placed in a combined fifth–sixth grade instead of a standard fifth. She finished tests first and read beyond the assigned pages. Numbers arranged themselves for her, but not in the approved sequence. Having attended three different third grades, she had never memorized the multiplication tables. She calculated silently and arrived at correct answers, yet when instructed to show her work she found there was nothing visible to display. The answer appeared whole. The path to it dissolved.

The teacher, Mr. Klien, was six foot six. When he stood in the doorway, he blocked the light. He had once been a social worker and knew Eleanor from the custody petition for Billy. Eleanor had not obtained custody. The marriage to Hugh had not been legal; the papers from Ray Parks were separation, not divorce. When Claire was nine, Eleanor and Hugh went before a judge and married quietly. No announcement followed. Claire continued to believe the wedding preceded her.

Mr. Klien said his wife taught art. He mentioned this more than once. He rested his arm across the shoulders of girls when he leaned down to review their papers. His sleeve brushed the back of Claire's neck. The gesture was casual and prolonged. It resembled something she had filed away under Eddie. Lilly, who sat two rows over, said in a low voice that Mr. Klien had tried to kiss her near the supply closet. Claire adjusted her routes accordingly. She made sure to never be alone in a room with him.

One evening Hugh returned from the bar before Claire had gone to bed. His face was arranged differently. He and Eleanor spoke in the other room while Claire sat at the kitchen table drawing. When they entered together, the air shifted.

"Has Eddie ever touched you in a bad way?" Eleanor asked. Hugh stood beside her.

Claire stood up and faced the sink instead of looking at her parents.

The enamel was chipped near the drain. She understood the question. "Yes," she said.

Silence accumulated.

The following day at school the desks remained aligned, the bell rang on schedule. At home Eddie's name was not mentioned. On Saturday morning a man she did not know walked through the house, opening closets and looking into corners as if taking inventory. He carried a clipboard. He handed Eleanor an envelope and left.

Later Eleanor and Hugh sat side by side at the kitchen table and said, "Do you want to go for a ride?" They were smiling in excess of the occasion. "We might not be back for a while. Bring some things."

Claire took the small red suitcase she had owned for as long as she could remember. She packed her jewelry, two books, a sweater. She clicked the clasp shut. The piano remained against the wall. The furniture stayed in place. Milk waited in the refrigerator.

They drove away from Dryden Street and did not return.

PART THREE

Hugh and Eleanor had packed their things and left. Nothing was explained. Eddie stayed where he was. No one spoke to Claire about Eddie. Claire did not bring him up. His name was not used again. He was still in Baltimore, still living in Maggie's house. Claire understood that something had been said which could not be taken back.

Claire sat between Eleanor and Hugh. The backseat was packed tight with suitcases and taped cardboard boxes. Hugh drove. The car hummed over the highway, tires ticking across the seams in the pavement. Brown signs for parks. Green for exits. Blue for gas. The land lay flat for miles, then gathered into low hills. Maryland and Pennsylvania receded behind them. New York lay ahead. Aunt Addie's apartment waited somewhere in Rochester.

They found the building and climbed the interior stairs to the second floor. On the landing, just outside Addie's door, stood a life-sized child doll—nearly three feet tall. It wore a red beret, red sweater, matching skirt, white ruffled socks, and black patent leather shoes. Addie had crocheted the outfit herself and positioned the doll carefully, as if it were standing guard.

Inside, the apartment looked much the same as it had in Pennsylvania. Floral prints. An oilcloth tablecloth in the kitchen. Crocheted afghans folded over the backs of chairs. The rooms felt familiar to Hugh. Not to Claire.

Ramona was there with a new man and her daughter, Tammy. Tammy was eight. Curly blonde hair. Blue eyes that caught and held the light. Eleanor had called her pretty. Hugh had said, "I like that kid." "Teeny, this is your cousin Tammy."

Claire watched the way Addie looked at Tammy—the steady, softened gaze reserved for something precious and easily damaged. Claire was taller now. Older. Her dark hair fell straight to her shoulders. Brown eyes, like the Deveraux side of the family. She felt the difference between them without putting it into words.

In the next room Ramona and the man began arguing. Their voices rose and broke against each other. Ramona struck his chest with her fist and shouted, "You black-necked bastard!" Addie kept her eyes on what she was doing. Someone laughed too loudly. Claire had never heard the phrase before. She stayed still.

The adults told the girls to go play.

Tammy pulled down a coloring book and a box of crayons. Claire chose a bird. She peeled back the paper on a crayon and the waxy smell lifted into the air. They colored carefully at first, then more quickly, talking and laughing.

Tammy brought out Candy Land. Claire thought it was meant for younger children. She played anyway. The cards slid across the table in bright colors. She watched the light catch in Tammy's hair, the slight tilt of her head when she smiled at nothing in particular.

From the kitchen Ramona's voice sharpened and then lowered. A man's voice answered. Something struck the floor. A pause. Then laughter again—thinner this time. The adults moved around the sound as though nothing had happened.

Claire advanced her piece one square at a time.
In the kitchen chairs scraped. Eleanor told Addie about Baltimore. Addie's hands moved across the table as she listened. "I can get you a job where I work," Addie said. "Waitress. The restaurant at the Ramada Inn off the highway." "That would be good," Eleanor said.

Hugh sat at the table with a short brown bottle of Genesee beer. In Baltimore he had drunk National Bohemian from long-necked bottles and sung altered versions of the jingle to make them laugh. He did not sing now.

The Boston Strangler had been in the news for months. Addie worried aloud that "the strangler will come around here." She was afraid of being attacked. One afternoon Hugh hid in the basement laundry room. When Addie came down with a basket of clothes he jumped out and made her scream. They both laughed hard.

Eleanor shook her head. "They get on my nerves with all that playing around."

Eleanor began work at the Ramada restaurant. Hugh found construction work. As soon as the first paychecks came, Eleanor and Hugh rented their own apartment. They did not stay long.

Sometimes Claire waited at the restaurant while Eleanor finished her shift. Addie was there too, both of them in pink uniforms, wiping tables and counting tips. They spoke about the hotel guests and where they had traveled from.

Claire sat alone in a booth. A white paper placemat showed a map of the highway, the hotel's name printed in red. She traced the roads with a pen, drawing lines that crossed and doubled back, creating new routes that did not exist.

It was decided they would move to Buffalo. There was better construction work there for Hugh.

Claire was on her way to her third sixth grade.

53 Buffalo

Hugh no longer looked directly at Claire when he spoke. He did not joke with her or include her in Scrabble or Rummy the way he had before. When he came into a room she moved aside so he could pass.

Before Buffalo he had talked to her about things he noticed—a crossword puzzle word or something he had found in the gutter while walking. Now he spoke only when something was required. When it came, the beating came without warning and ended without words.

Eleanor seemed older than she had in Baltimore. In the evenings she moved from room to room putting things back in place. The house did not stay in order. She sat down often and rubbed her eyes with the heel of her hand. Claire saw her sitting alone at the kitchen table, reading cards, laying them out in the patterns she always used. Eleanor kept the house going. She told Claire what needed to be done and corrected her when she forgot.

In Buffalo, Claire no longer listened for Eddie's step in the hall or the sound of his voice in the next room. She could close a door and know it would stay closed. Still, she moved as if someone might be listening.

Eleanor found work in a family-owned bakery. Not baking. Cleaning, organizing, moving trays. The bakery filled the first floor of a three-story brick building. Above it were apartments and art studios with tall windows. Eleanor and Hugh rented one of the upstairs apartments.

There were other small businesses on the block. A produce stand. A drugstore. The neighborhood was near the university. Professors and other professionals lived on the wide side streets in large houses with porches and trimmed hedges. Claire went to school with their children.

She arrived with six weeks left in sixth grade. Her teacher told Eleanor the school was highly ranked. Claire had missed too much school. Her previous schools had been in Baltimore. They should not be surprised, he said, if she had to repeat the grade. Because the year was nearly over, her report card would depend on final exams. The tests covered everything the class had learned since September.

Claire listened in class. The material was not new. When the teacher asked questions, she knew the answers. She did not raise her hand as often as she once had. The other students spoke easily. Their hands went up without hesitation.

The teacher suggested speech therapy. Claire went to the small office at the end of the hall. A woman asked her to say, "The red rooster ran around the corner." Then other sentences, careful and bright. The woman listened and shook her head.

"She doesn't need therapy," she told the teacher and Eleanor. "She has a Baltimore accent."

This surprised Claire. Eleanor worked to smooth her own speech. On Dryden Street children said "zink" for "sink" and "wooder" for "water". Claire and Eleanor did not. Hugh's voice carried western Pennsylvania—flat and rural. It sounded nothing like Baltimore to her.

The children in her class were polite. They talked about ski trips and summers at lake houses. Vacations in Europe. Claire listened.

During a discussion on Civil Rights, the teacher called on her without warning. "Claire, you're from the South. Tell us your view on race." She had not raised her hand. She said everyone should have the same opportunities. That a person should be judged by behavior, not color. The teacher made an almost imperceptible dismissive wave. "Oh—face, not race." He moved on.

The girls dressed differently. Claire still wore dresses with full skirts and a bow at the back. Corrective Mary Jane shoes with stiff straps. No one else dressed this way. She was old enough to see it. Some of the girls had started wearing bras. Claire had one now too. Several of them had gotten their first period. She waited for hers and said nothing when the others talked about it.

The other girls wore straight shift dresses and soft flat shoes. When she admired a pair, the girl said, "They're Pappagallos." A name, said as if it explained everything. Claire repeated it silently so she would remember.

Exams were given over a week. She had never taken anything called an exam before. When the first paper was placed on her desk, she saw it was only a test. Questions. Blank lines. She wrote her answers and carried the paper to the teacher's desk before anyone else stood up. He looked at her as if she might have misunderstood. She had not. Test. Answers. Finished.

For several days it continued. On some exams a few students finished before she did. She kept track without meaning to. Her promotion to seventh grade rested on these scores. They would get their grades next week. Claire waited.

99, 98, 97, 94. English, History, Science, Math.
In September Claire would begin seventh grade at the junior high school
in Buffalo.

The entire sixth-grade class was invited to a birthday party for Peter
and Pamela: twins, turning twelve and graduating elementary school.
Claire went.

When Eleanor took her shopping this time, Claire chose the dress
herself—a madras plaid shift. It looked like something the other girls
would wear. Not too young. Not strange. She would look right.

Pam sometimes spoke to Claire at lunch. Boys and girls did not mix
much at school, but Pete was polite and Claire thought he was cute. All
the children at this school were polite. Some seemed to like her. Some did
not. It was hard to tell. No one was openly unkind.

Getting ready, Claire put on the white Keds she had insisted on.
Eleanor had hesitated—the soles were thin, not practical—but Claire
knew. The shoes mattered. She added a wide, soft headband that matched
the dress. In the mirror she saw what she had been aiming for. This time
she looked right.

Eleanor hovered in the doorway, smoothing the air. "If they say
something you don't understand, just smile and nod." She adjusted the
headband though it did not need adjusting. Claire nodded but did not
plan to smile and nod at everything.

The party was at the twins' house. It was large, like most of the
houses in that neighborhood—broad front steps, trimmed hedges, windows
that caught the late afternoon light. Most of Claire's classmates did not
know she lived in an apartment above a bakery. They did not know
Eleanor worked downstairs. They were unaware that her father drank, or
that sometimes he used his belt. They did not know why the family had
left Baltimore.

During the party, the twins' older sister passed through the room on
her way out. She and another older girl stood near the doorway, talking.
Claire listened the way she always did—quietly, without appearing to.
They were discussing something called a cotillion. The word was said as if

everyone should already understand it. Claire stored it away. She would ask later.

There were games. Cake. Claire followed along, watching first, then moving when it seemed correct to move. Nothing went wrong. It was pleasant. Not remarkable.

Eleanor arrived at the agreed time. They walked home together. Eleanor asked many questions—who was there, what did they serve, did anyone say anything interesting. Claire answered what seemed necessary. Then she asked about the cotillion.

Eleanor's eyes widened. A coming-out party, she said. A formal presentation. White dresses, gloves, a ballroom. Only the right families. She described the gowns in detail, how they flared at the waist, how the skirts brushed the floor. It was an event of standing. Of class.

Eleanor spoke for some time.

Claire listened, but her thoughts had already drifted elsewhere.

Hugh still took them out on Sundays. The roads were rural, unmarked. Dun-colored gravel and dust. The tires made a steady crunch.

A small sign stood at the edge of a dirt road: "Bell Aerosystems – Private Property". Hugh slowed but did not turn around. Something moved in the distance beyond a low corrugated building.

Eleanor leaned forward. "Look, Teen."

A man rose into the air with a metal pack strapped to his back. He lifted straight up, then angled and crossed the road in front of them. The sound followed after. Claire stared. Earlier that year, John Glenn had orbited the earth. Now a man flew over their windshield. Hugh said it must be the experimental jet pack he had read about.

They watched until a man stepped out of the building and walked toward the car. His jaw was set. He asked who they were and what they were doing there. Hugh said they were a family out for a Sunday drive. The man looked into the back seat, then back at Hugh. He said the jet pack was still in testing and the facility was not open to the public. They would have to leave. They turned the car around.

Another weekend, they drove toward the Iroquois Reservation. Eleanor, as always, brought up her Iroquois blood, her great-grandmother's trunk of beaded clothing and moccasins. Hugh said he had found arrow-heads in fields when he was a boy.

They found a small store near the edge of the reservation. Claire bought a beaded owl with a safety pin sewn to the back. She fastened it to her sweater.

Sometimes Addie, Ramona, and Tammy came along. Once they all drove to Niagara Falls. Claire sat in the front between Hugh and Eleanor. Tammy rode in the back with Addie and Ramona. Claire and Tammy leaned over the seat until the adults stopped the car and changed the arrangement.

At the border a guard leaned into the driver's window and asked where they were from. Addie, Hugh and Ramona named the small town near the farm where Hugh had grown up. Eleanor said, "Baltimore."
In the backseat, Claire showed Tammy how to fold silver chewing gum

wrappers into chains. They chewed quickly and saved the foil. The chain grew across their laps.

At the falls Hugh said the Canadian side was prettier. They walked through tunnels beneath the water and came out again into the roar. The falling water forced air upward in hard gusts. Spray struck their faces and soaked their clothes. Claire and Tammy climbed onto the guardrail while Hugh and Ramona held them by the backs of their jackets.

Eleanor bent close to Claire's ear. "Remember this," she said. "It is one of the seven wonders of the world."

Lunches packed, Abby and Claire rode their bikes to the cemetery. They ate under the trees where it was quiet. That was their favorite place.

After moving to Buffalo, Claire discovered a neighborhood around the corner from the commercial strip near their apartment. It was not like Dryden Street in Baltimore. The houses were similar to one another—large Victorian clapboard homes with deep porches and wide lawns. Turrets. Gables. Long driveways leading to detached garages. Paint in muted, deliberate colors. Curtains open in the afternoon; lace held back with cords. The paint was fresh but never bright. The porches were swept, but Claire never saw anyone sweeping them. The hedges were trimmed square. Nothing sagged. Nothing peeled.

There were several girls her age. She learned which doors she could knock on. Abby lived in a house in the middle of the block. They grew close quickly. Both had long dark hair. Both played piano. Both had faces that made adults lean forward and ask, "What's wrong?" Neither answered the question.

Abby's father was never there. Abby said he was away "on sabbatical." Claire kept the word to look up later. Abby's mother was never visible when Claire visited, though Abby referred to her often. The references felt precise, as if someone were just upstairs. They did not go above the first floor.

The house was large compared to the row houses Claire had known in Baltimore. Dark wood framed the rooms. Patterned rugs lay over polished floors. A Steinway grand piano stood in the living room, like the ones at Peabody where Claire had taken lessons. The kitchen had black-and-white tile, tall cabinets, and a stove with six burners. The refrigerator and pantry were full. Although Claire never saw anyone else, there was always food.

One afternoon they decided to make fudge. Claire recited Eleanor's recipe from memory—sugar, cocoa, milk. The pan was smaller than the one at home, but everything fit. That seemed close enough. The mixture came to a boil. Claire watched for the soft-ball stage, a drop falling into cold water and forming a small sphere. Abby stood by with the glass of water while Claire held the spoon. Without warning, the surface bubbled, thickened, lifted, then surged over the rim. Boiling chocolate spread across the stovetop and hissed. They turned off the burner. The syrup ran toward the edges and began to set. It was too hot to touch. "It's all right," Abby said. "Someone will clean it." They left it.

They packed their lunches in paper bags and rode to the cemetery. The stones stood in rows, names and dates carved deep. Claire liked the way the light moved across the stones. Shadows lengthened and slid. The carved letters filled with gold and then went dark again. They sat under a large tree and got comfortable.

The afternoons came and went.

One day Claire rode to Abby's house and found it closed. Windows shut though the weather was warm. No bikes in the yard. She knocked. No answer.

She returned the next day. And the next. Nothing changed. The curtains stayed drawn. The driveway stayed empty.

After a while she stopped going daily. She checked now and then. One day a woman answered the door. She spoke with an accent and said they were from Switzerland. She smiled and invited Claire inside. She called for her daughter.

The house was lighter. There was more space between the furniture. The rugs lay flatter. The air moved differently. The Steinway was still in the living room.

The daughter came forward with long blond braids. She looked younger than Claire expected. They sat together for a few minutes. Suddenly the girl stood up straight and said, carefully, "May I please go the bathroom sir?" Claire blinked. Then she nodded. "Yes." The girl disappeared down the hall.

Claire stayed a little longer. The woman offered her something to drink. The rooms felt open, rearranged but intact.

The daughter was seven. She was polite and earnest. Claire had nothing to say to her. She said her mother was expecting her and rode home.

The apartment in Buffalo had a piano, but it was not hers.

Eleanor rented a spinet for the living room. It was short and plain, pushed against the wall. Claire played what she was assigned and closed the lid.

On Dryden Street there had been her upright with worn keys and carved details. She lingered over it, playing on, from her books and from memory.

Her things were arranged in the room. The stuffed animals lined the bed; some had been with her since she was very small. Her suitcase stayed in the closet. She sat on the edge of the bed for a moment, listening to the clatter and smells from the bakery below, imagining the streets around the corner.

Later, she walked around the corner. The houses were bigger here, with clipped hedges and shiny doorknobs. Stacy came into view, jodhpurs and tall black boots, a helmet tucked under her arm. She smelled faintly of leather. They went into Stacy's house together. Her mother hovered nearby, insisting, "Have one of Mrs. Bellagamba's meatballs! You cannot come here and not have one of Mrs. Bellagamba's meatballs." She said her own name each time.

Claire remembered once sitting on a horse, led in a slow circle in a yard in South Carolina. She did not mention it.

She went to other houses.

Eloise lived near Abby's old house. After Abby was gone, Claire sometimes went there instead.

There were eight children in Eloise's family. The house was large. A small door beneath the staircase opened into a narrow room with no windows. The children called it the secret room. They hid there.

They had a miniature schnauzer named Hans. He had a pedigree. He was going to be a show dog.

Eloise was younger than Claire. She had every toy Claire had seen advertised on television and others Claire had not. A Chatty Cathy doll lay on her bed. When you pulled the string in its back it said, "Read me a story." "Please change my dress." "I love you."

Her baby brother had a small electric car, large enough to sit inside. The family stood in the driveway while he steered in careful circles.

"Look at him in the Stutz Bearcat!" they said.

Claire did not know what that was.

Eloise's mother smiled at everyone the same way. The older children smiled too. The house was always bright. Voices rose and overlapped. It was closer to television than any house Claire had been inside.

When she left, she felt tired.

One afternoon she was alone in the apartment and thought about Eloise's house. She did not want to speak to Eloise. She dialed the number anyway.

"Hello?" Eloise's mother said.

Claire held the receiver and said nothing.

"Hello?" The voice grew louder. Then the line went dead.

Claire set the phone back in its cradle.

She called again on another day. And again. Each time she said nothing. Each time the mother waited longer before hanging up.

One afternoon the mother answered.

"Hello?"

Silence.

"Claire? Is that you?"

Claire hung up.

She did not call again.

"Beatniks," Hugh said about the young couple across the hall. Eleanor agreed.

The man had a beard. He wore jeans and dark sunglasses, even in the hallway. The woman's hair was long and straight and very blond. She worked as a waitress at the coffee shop two blocks away. People called it the Beatnik place.

Once, their door stood open for a moment. Claire saw a large abstract painting on an easel. Thick shapes. Heavy color. Then the door shut.

She would have liked to know them. They were adults. That was the end of it.

The building held apartments, the bakery on the corner, and a large studio with north light. The artist was Gabor Kovacs. He was older. Clean-shaven. He made careful drawings of faces and hands and taught classes at night.

One afternoon Eleanor stepped inside with Claire. "We live down the hall," she said.

Kovacs wiped his hands on a rag and showed them the room. Easels stood in rows. Charcoal dust lay in a tray beneath a drawing board. Light filled the windows and stayed there.

He studied Claire. "She could model for the class sometime" he said. Claire stood beside Eleanor and did not move.

On television, beatniks snapped their fingers and leaned against brick walls. Maynard G. Krebs on *The Many Loves of Dobie Gillis* rolled his eyes at the word "work." He played the bongos. He drifted.

The people across the hall carried groceries. They shut their door quietly. They went to work.

Claire had noticed that television was often wrong about people.

On Saturdays she walked to her music lesson and passed the coffee shop. Posters of places she did not know hung in the window. Small round tables stood inside. In the morning it was closed. Chairs tipped upside down on tabletops.

She slowed as she passed. Looked in. Then kept walking.

That evening she went to a classmate's garage for a Halloween party.

Everyone wore a costume. Claire had chosen Beatnik. Eleanor helped, as she always did. Black tights. Keds. Hugh's white dress shirt, long enough to be a dress. A black beret from the back of a drawer. Claire's hair needed nothing done to it. It already hung straight with bangs across her forehead. There were ghosts and a cat with painted whiskers. Zorro. A hula girl in a grass skirt. Rocky and Bullwinkle costumes from a store.

Claire stood among them in black and white.

It did not feel like a costume.

"Rewind, and let's hear that again, Claire!"

Diane was Eleanor's boss's daughter. Same age as Claire, but at a different school. On days off school, her parents brought her to the bakery. Sometimes they paid the girls to fold cake boxes. With their pay they went next door to the soda fountain. They looked into the mirror behind the counter while they sipped their sodas and talked about how in Baltimore a soda was a coke, but in Buffalo a Coke was a pop and a soda has ice cream in it. Sometimes they went upstairs to Claire's to play. Claire liked how their laughter filled the quiet corners of the apartment.

Eleanor and Hugh had bought Claire a portable tape recorder. The girls played their favorite records and sang into the microphone. Diane had short blonde hair and a good voice. When she sang "He's a Rebel," Claire said, "You sound just like the record." She noticed the way Diane's eyes lit up when she hit the high notes.

They had a lot in common. Clothes they liked. The same kinds of toys. Stuffed animal collections. Coke floats dripping onto paper napkins. Peppermint patties sticking to their fingers. Both took piano lessons at Field's Music School. Eleanor had signed Claire up at Diane's parents' suggestion. Straight up Elmwood Avenue, about six blocks. Nothing like Peabody. The only thing Claire liked about it was that Diane went there too.

Claire practiced what she was told. She didn't like the rented spinet. The notes came out flat and small, but she knew Eleanor had sacrificed for it, so she kept at it. She went to her classes. She took music theory in a large room with other kids. On the first day, a short, fat bald man with glasses hummed a note. "Can anyone tell me what note that was?" Two students raised their hands. Both wrong. Claire thought C, but she didn't raise hers. She felt the note hover in the room, waiting for someone brave enough to claim it.

After class there was a reception. Parents, teachers, students. Kool-aid and cookies. The paper cups stuck together, then came apart. The table was damp. Claire told Eleanor about the note. Eleanor marched over to the teacher. Claire stayed still beside her, wishing she could fold herself into the corner. Wishing Eleanor wasn't so eager. The teacher hummed again. "Alright, what is this note?" Claire thought G. "G?" Her face warmed.

"It was G," he said. "But you don't seem sure. You might have perfect pitch." He looked past Eleanor, around the room, over Claire's head. Claire wanted to leave, the voices pressing at the back of her neck, the hum of the note still in her ears.

They went home.

60 Report Card

Junior high in Buffalo was different from elementary school. Students changed classrooms. Lockers lined the halls. Bells cut the day into pieces. Claire had a homeroom teacher, Mr. Diamond. He also taught English.

Corporal punishment was allowed. Claire had never attended a school where teachers were permitted to hit students. In Baltimore, that belonged to Catholic schools.

Mr. Diamond was a short man who wore a suit and tie every day. He carried a drum mallet as he walked between the desks. If he did not like what he saw on a paper, he tapped the back of a student's head with the padded end. The sound was dull and practiced.

He never hit Claire.

She watched him and thought: Barbaric.

One afternoon he focused on a tall boy named Gary Chen. He called Gary to the front of the room and told him to get on his hands and knees. Then he stacked textbooks across Gary's back. "Stay," he said. Gary stayed.

The class went on.

Claire could not follow the lesson. She watched Gary's shoulders tremble under the weight.

After school she told Eleanor.

"If he lays a hand on my child, I will tear him limb from limb," Eleanor said.

She made an appointment.

At the meeting Eleanor told Mr. Diamond never to touch Claire. He studied her face and said he never hit the girls.

Eleanor reported this back as fact.

Claire sat with the information. The boys were still hit. The mallet still moved between desks.

There were other classes. Biology. Art. She liked those rooms. She had once liked English. Now she answered questions precisely and kept her eyes on her paper.

After a few months, the first report cards of the year came out.

The usual A's lined the page. Then a B in math.

Claire felt it land. She kept her face still.

At school the other kids compared grades. They were pleased with B's. Some waved their report cards in the air. Claire listened. Maybe it wasn't so bad.

She took it home.

Eleanor studied the paper. "You could do better on the math."

They ate dinner. Hugh came home before Claire went to bed. Eleanor handed him the report card.

He called Claire into the kitchen.

He spoke slowly. Carefully. Each word placed down hard. He sat very straight, as if steadiness could pass for something else. The smell of alcohol sat on him.

He wanted her to argue.

Something in the scene tilted. One B among A's. He tried to make his voice heavy with importance. It struck her as absurd.

"It's still better than most of the other kids," she said.

He stood up at once and pulled his belt from the loops.

Claire ran into the living room. He followed. The belt snapped through the air and found her back, her legs. Again. Again. Eleanor stood near the doorway and chewed her fingernails.

Claire twisted away. "You're a drunk," she said.

He took off one boot and threw it. It missed. He pulled off the other and threw again. The heel struck her thigh.

The room narrowed.

She went into the bedroom, shut the door, and threw herself onto the bed. She cried into the pillow until her face felt hot and swollen.

Later she asked Eleanor why he had beaten her so hard for one B.

Eleanor said, "Addie said he should beat you more. You have a smart mouth."

Claire lay still.

In that moment she hated Hugh.

She already did not like Addie. She would never like her.

Claire walked into social studies on Friday after lunch. The usual chatter. Everyone settled into their seats. The teacher stood at the front, crying. Her hair was in its usual updo. Her eyes were red. She held a tissue. Everyone went quiet. She motioned for the class to sit.

"The president has been shot."

She sniffed. Wiped her eyes. Her voice was muffled, as if she had been crying for a while. She explained that John F. Kennedy had been assassinated in a motorcade in Dallas, Texas. School was dismissed early. Seeing the teacher so upset was unsettling. Hearing the president was murdered was a shock. The students left quickly.

Claire walked into the apartment. Eleanor was at the ironing board. The television spoke about the assassination. Claire asked questions about presidents. She knew Eisenhower had been president before Kennedy. She asked who had been the best president.

"FDR," Eleanor said. "Lincoln too. Kennedy was very good. Sad about him dying." She worried about Russia and nuclear war.

Claire remembered drills at school—hiding under desks. Now they weren't told to hide. They were told to walk home.

The next week was Thanksgiving. Eleanor roasted a duck. Hugh didn't like turkey. Their meals seemed small compared to the feasts on television. Even in elementary school, they hadn't had turkey—usually duck or capon. Hugh liked to tell the story from second grade. The teacher had asked if everyone ate turkey. Claire said no.

"What did you have instead?"

"A chicken that will never be a father."

The teacher pressed her lips together. Later she told Eleanor. It became one of Hugh's favorites. He was the one who described a capon that way when Claire had asked what it was.

This Thanksgiving there were no funny stories. The whole country was supposed to be in mourning. They watched the carriage with six white horses. The black riderless horse. Boots backward in the stirrups. Three-year-old John-John saluting his father's flag-draped casket.

Hugh and Eleanor talked about moving. Claire didn't catch the details but was told she and Eleanor would visit Baltimore over Christmas break. Hugh would stay in Buffalo.

Christmas in Buffalo was small. The tree was fake, small, on a table-top. Eleanor took pictures of an unsmiling Claire in front of it.

They went on a Greyhound bus. They came back. Hugh wasn't home. The apartment looked the same but felt different. Claire went to her room. Her stuffed animals were gone.

"Where are they?" she asked Eleanor.

"I don't know," Eleanor said.

When Hugh came home, Eleanor found out. "Hugh gave them to the Salvation Army. He said he thought you were too old for stuffed toys."

Claire cried.

The girls stood behind the school building while junior high was in session. The other students were around front in the designated area. Claire talked with a girl she had known slightly at Clement School and three others. One of the girls smoked a cigarette, passing it between fingers without looking down. They were all in seventh grade. Claire kept her hands in her sleeves.

Hugh, Eleanor, and Claire were back in South Baltimore, in another furnished apartment. Like the others, not the Dryden Street house from sixth grade. No piano. No Billy or Bucky.

Maggie and Eddie had separated. Maggie worked at a bank and lived in an apartment in Highlandtown with her two sons. Eddie worked as a guard at the penitentiary. No one said why they split up, or what had happened to Eddie's job as a teacher.

Hugh was building bridges again with Leroy at the construction company that always hired them. Doris was spoken of in the past tense.

Eleanor had taken the test for a high school equivalency certificate and was waiting for the results.

Claire was not the same as the last time they lived in South Baltimore. She had grown used to people being polite, even when they did not care for you. Here, in her second seventh grade, the children were louder. If they disliked someone they said so, or shoved them, or hit them. Arriving in the middle of the school year did not help.

One girl she had known at Clement School accepted her, and that girl's friends were polite, but to everyone else Claire was new.

She wore a beige trench coat, a pleated black watch plaid kilt fastened with a large gold pin, and a soft sweater. She did not know yet that this made her noticeable.

Between classes, on the crowded stairs, a boy said something to her. She heard the tone more than the words. Then a spitting sound. When she reached the classroom, the girl from Clement School came up behind her.

"Somebody spit pumpkin seeds all over your back."

Claire pulled off her cardigan and looked. Chewed pumpkin seeds clung to the fabric. Some were caught in her hair. She managed not to cry or gag.

She told Eleanor so she would not get in trouble for the clothes. Eleanor said things would change again soon.

Hugh had a few paychecks by then. Eleanor passed the equivalency test and began looking for work. She also began looking for another place to live, somewhere with a better school.

The new place was in Northeast Baltimore. The apartment was the entire second floor of a large house, with one extra room on the third. It was not furnished.

The landlady lived downstairs. Eleanor said Mrs. Cooper was seventy-five. She was small and bent, with thin gray hair pulled into a bun.

Mrs. Cooper was raising her granddaughter Audrey, who was older than Claire. They lived mostly on the first floor, but their bedrooms were on the third floor, across from the extra room that went with the Young's apartment. It was a house, not an apartment building. There was less privacy than usual.

There was a large backyard, and Puddles was there again. Eleanor had left the little black-and-white corgi with someone while they were in New York and had brought her back.

Claire was glad to see Puddles. Puddles stayed close to her people. Hugh built a small house for her in the yard. Sometimes she was allowed inside.

Claire enrolled in her third seventh grade.

Franklin Junior High School.

63 Light

Their new apartment, upstairs from Mrs. Cooper, was on a narrow side street lined with large clapboard houses. Some were duplexes. Each house had a porch. Trees shaded the sidewalks.

The Young family were the only renters.

This place had more light than their old apartments. The ocean painting they had had since Claire was a baby hung on the kitchen wall.

Betty lived two doors down. Claire spent most afternoons there.

Eleanor took Claire to visit Maggie at her new apartment. Maggie laughed a lot. She talked about her job at the bank and showed them the high heels she planned to wear when she went out dancing with the girls from work.

She did not talk about Eddie.

Eleanor and Maggie sat close together and spoke quietly while Claire played with Maggie's little boys, Johnny and Eddie Jr.

At school Claire made friends quickly. During lunch break they stood together in the school yard and talked. One day Claire felt someone looking at her. She turned and saw Eddie standing across the narrow street. He was wearing his old jacket and the glasses he sometimes wore. Her stomach dropped.

He was staring at her. Then he laughed.

She turned back to the girls and kept talking. When she looked again he was gone.

After school she rode the bus home.

As soon as Eleanor came in from work Claire told her she had seen Eddie.

Eleanor said some girls had complained about Eddie when he was a student teacher, but no one had believed them. He had never gotten a full-time teaching job. Now he was working as a guard at the prison. Claire said she wanted to tell someone that the other girls had been telling the truth. Eleanor said she did not want to go to the police.

"I don't want to put you through that."

Claire did not understand. It seemed better to tell, so he would not hurt any more girls. Eleanor's face turned red. She said it was time for

Claire to go to bed.

A few days later there was news.

The eight-year-old daughter of Eddie's landlord had told on him. The police came, but Eddie convinced them the girl was lying.

He moved to another place.

Eleanor told Hugh that Eddie had been seen near Claire's school.

Claire saw the look on Hugh's face and the tightness in his shoulders. She knew he was thinking about going after Eddie.

If he did that he would go to jail.

Claire said, "Eddie should kill himself. It would solve everything."

Eleanor called the police and told them Eddie had been seen watching Claire at school. The police searched Eddie's car. They found little girls' clothing in the trunk. They were on their way to arrest him.

Maggie telephoned, crying. The police had found Eddie in his apartment. Bullet through the temple. His service weapon on the floor next to his body.

Eleanor told Claire, "Eddie shot himself."

Claire felt relieved.

"Tell people it was an accident," Eleanor said, as if it were settled, as if Claire should rehearse it. "He was cleaning his rifle and it went off."

Maggie said the same thing. Everyone said the same thing.

It was a lie.

Claire had said he should kill himself, and he did. She thought it was justice for the things he had done. The world was safer without him.

She did not like lying.

Maggie played the widow with two small children. Her dark hair in a soft bouffant. A pillbox hat. A tailored suit. She talked as if she and Eddie had never separated. As if he had never hurt anyone.

When Claire's name came up, Maggie rolled her eyes.

People expressed condolences. They held Maggie's hand and patted the back of it.

"Oh I'm so sorry. Let me know if I can do anything to help you and the boys."

In the family album on Maggie's living room table, Claire had been cut out of the photographs. Sometimes only her face, if she stood in the middle of a group.

There were no pictures of Claire.

Many pictures of Eddie. Eddie with the boys. Eddie and Maggie dressed up to go out.

When Claire asked why she had been cut out, Maggie said, "You were a terrible child."

Maggie visited more after Eddie died. She brought the boys and sat in the kitchen talking with Eleanor. Eleanor had been sixteen when Maggie was born. They looked like sisters.

Maggie talked about Hugh. His drinking. The rural area where he grew up. She talked about Ray too, as if he had been a wonderful husband and father.

She did not talk about Eleanor's bruises. She did not talk about the women Ray went off with.

Sometimes Maggie took Claire with her to shop or to get their hair done.

"Cut it all off," Maggie said to Mr. Richard.

According to Maggie, Mr. Richard was a famous hairdresser. Maggie told him to cut Claire's almost waist-length hair so she would look more mature.

Claire did not want it cut. She let Maggie and Mr. Richard decide.

When he finished, Mr. Richard pulled off the salon cape with a flourish and spun the chair toward the mirror. He smiled and winked.

"Now you look like a teenager."

Claire did not like what she saw.

Maggie came over and stood behind her. She used the high voice Eleanor sometimes used—the one for pets and for people you wanted to fool.

"Perfect," she said to Claire's reflection. "This changes your image completely."

Claire hated it.

At home Eleanor said it looked fine. She praised Maggie for taking Claire to the salon.

Hugh said he didn't like the haircut when someone asked. After that he said nothing.

When Claire went to Betty's house, Betty stared. Her eyes widened. Her mouth opened.

"What happened?"

Claire told her.

Betty said, "What was she thinking? It looks like a mushroom on your head."

Claire spent the next year trying to make her hair grow faster.

Claire went to Betty's house nearly every day after school. At school they hardly spoke; they passed each other without stopping. School, Betty's house, Maggie's apartment, home —Separate worlds.

Betty lived with her grandparents, Mr. and Mrs. Carpenter, in a three-story house with a deep backyard. Mr. Carpenter had built a fish pond edged with stones, and a sun porch served as a playroom. Furniture was soft and plentiful, lamps and side tables in every room.

The grandparents ruled mostly from the top floor and the kitchen. Betty's mother, Carmen, had a bedroom and a small living room on the second floor. Betty's room and her little brother's room ran down the same hall.

Mrs. Carpenter cooked large meals every day—meat, vegetables, sauces, relishes, side dishes, all at once. There was always plenty.

Betty was big. So were the others. Carmen and Mrs. Carpenter talked to her about losing weight. She didn't care. Eleanor sometimes called her "fat Betty," the way someone might say tall Betty or red-haired Betty. She liked her. Everyone did.

Two doors down was the Fisher house. Mr. Fisher was a retired policeman. His old K-9 dog, Pistol, lived there with Mr. Fisher's mother, his nephew Danny, and a few foster boys who had spent time at the reform school out in Baltimore County at the same time as Danny.

Once Claire went to knock on the Fishers' door. Pistol jumped against the glass storm door. The glass shattered and hit Claire across the stomach. The dog cut his leg on the broken pieces. Mr. Fisher shouted at Claire while he put Pistol into the back seat of his car and drove to the animal hospital. The dog healed, but after that Mr. Fisher never liked Claire.

Danny Fisher was Betty's boyfriend.

On weekends Claire and Betty played games on the sun porch and listened to the radio. Sometimes Claire spent the night. Betty told stories that made Claire say "Wow" or laugh out loud. They often played cards with Danny and sometimes with one of the foster boys. One of them, a boy called Ace, once hid in the bushes beside Claire's house and jumped out and kissed her. She had never been kissed before. She laughed and pulled away. He tried again another time and she pushed him back, still laughing. He laughed too and went home.

After that she paid closer attention to her cards and began beating him at Rummy. He stopped trying to kiss her.

Claire and Betty walked around the neighborhood, and Betty had a story about every house. The big house on the corner belonged to the Wolfes. Everyone there was tall. Sarah Wolfe was a senior in high school and six feet tall. Her brother William was a junior, six foot six, and played football for his school. Their mother was tall too. Their father had died when William was a baby.

The only one who was not tall was Aunt Millie. Millie had Down syndrome. She was short and round and always smiling. She liked visitors and helped with the cooking and housework. She could write her name.

Claire and Betty sometimes stopped in to visit. William Wolfe stayed around when they did and talked mostly about football. He was excited about playing in the City–Poly game at the stadium, the same place where the Colts played. One afternoon he saw Claire by herself and asked her to come sit on the back porch. She sat with him a long time while he talked. He put his arm around her and touched her face. He did not try to kiss her, and after a while she went home.

Dwayne lived next door to Claire. He went to Catholic school and wanted to be a photographer. He had a large camera and a darkroom in his basement. Sometimes he took pictures of Claire and the other neighbors outside, then printed them and handed them around. He wore a signet ring and belonged to something called DeMolay, which he mentioned often. When he spoke to Claire he turned red and stumbled over his words.

One day he asked Betty and Claire if they would go bowling with him and his friend Fred. Claire asked Eleanor, and Eleanor said it was fine. The girls went with them to the duckpin lanes on Harford Road and bowled several games. The bowling was fun. After that Dwayne suggested other things to do, but Claire said she could not go.

Most afternoons Claire went to Betty's. They sat on the sun porch and listened to the radio and played cards until it was time for Claire to go home.

Claire's thirteenth birthday was a pajama party at her house.

She was not used to people coming in. There had always been something to hide—Hugh drunk, worn furniture, a neighborhood people commented on. The apartment in Northeast Baltimore upstairs from Mrs. Cooper and Audrey required no explanations. Girls from school and nearby streets came without hesitation: some from larger houses with several siblings, some from apartments with one parent, some from houses where grandparents shared the rooms with parents and children.

Eleanor had managed a matching living-room set. Claire had her own bedroom with her own telephone extension.

Eight girls came. They stayed up late talking and laughing, telling ghost stories, playing records, making prank phone calls. There was cake and ice cream and a pile of wrapped presents. Each girl brought a record. No one had planned it. It was simply what they all wanted themselves, and what Claire would want. By some small stroke of luck there were no duplicates. The records played most of the night.

Eleanor had arranged things with Hugh. He stayed quiet and out of the way. He did not argue with Claire or fall asleep drunk where anyone could see him. His absence made the rooms easier.

Eleanor moved in and out, checking on them, then returning to the other room. Once or twice she came in when the noise rose too high for the hour.

Afterward Claire put the new records with the others and looked through the row of sleeves. The collection felt different now.

As she did every year, Eleanor gave Claire summer clothes for her birthday. School would be over in a month.

That summer Claire persuaded Hugh to nail two halves of an old roller skate to a board so she could skateboard. She had good balance and the street sloped gently downhill. Betty watched but did not try it. Dwayne came out with his camera and took pictures.

Some evenings, after everyone on the block had parked, the children stretched a badminton net across the narrow street and played. Sometimes the parents joined. When a car came, they pulled the net back and replaced it once it passed.

Claire went to the beach that summer. Their old neighbors from Dryden Street asked Eleanor if Claire could come with them to Ocean City to keep Elizabeth company for a long weekend.

This time Claire went without Eleanor and Hugh. She stayed in a motel, sharing a room with Elizabeth. They went to the amusement park on the boardwalk and played Whack-a-Mole and ring toss. They went through the Haunted Mansion and Claire rode the Gravitron without Elizabeth. It spun so fast the riders stuck to the wall before the floor dropped away. That was her favorite.

She bought a blue sweatshirt that said Ocean City across the front. It hung loose on her and came down to where her shorts stopped. Standing at the spin-art booth in her sweatshirt and Keds, with no one to supervise, she felt older. She squeezed paint onto the spinning paper. When it stopped, the attendant set the picture into a cardboard mat. Claire thought it was beautiful.

Elizabeth's family liked to get suntans. They rubbed baby oil on their arms and legs and lay in the sun. They put some on Claire and she spread her towel beside them.

By the time they returned to the hotel Claire's skin was bright red. Elizabeth stood at the mirror admiring her own tan skin and the pale streaks in her hair.

"You got sunburned," she said to Claire, wrinkling her nose, then added that it would turn into a tan.

It did not. By evening Claire saw large blisters on her shoulders, chest, and back. She felt hot and cold at the same time and could not stop shivering. She thought she might throw up.

No one seemed to understand how sick she felt. She went along with the plans. Her skin hurt and her head hurt and she wished she was home.

When they dropped her off Sunday afternoon Eleanor looked shocked. She laid cool wet cloths on the most painful places.

"We can't go in the sun like they do," she said. "We burn."

Claire watched her skin begin to peel. She wished she had known before she went to the beach.

67 Sorcerer's Apprentice

Eleanor got a job at the front counter of a dry cleaner in Northeast Baltimore. She walked to work and back and stood most of the day.

She had never been heavy, but now she was very lean, almost like a teenager, though still very feminine. She bought new clothes for the job and for her smaller size.

When clothes were not picked up for a year, the store kept them. The boss let the employees choose what they wanted and pay only the cleaning bill. Eleanor had an eye for quality. She brought home classic things she could never have afforded new. Sometimes she found things for Claire and even for Hugh.

She looked sharp. Always pressed, always matched. A scarf or pin set just right. She stood straighter when she dressed for work.

She examined herself the way she examined Claire, looking for faults. One day Claire said, "You're beautiful."

Eleanor smirked. "I used to be pretty. You don't look like me. I don't know who you look like… I think aliens implanted you in my uterus."

After her conversation with Claire, Eleanor went to the kitchen to get ready for visitors.

Eleanor was still friendly with some of the women from the sewing factory. Violet came most often. She was about ten years older than Eleanor and had a grown daughter named Poppy. They visited together or separately.

Not many people came to the apartment. Violet and Poppy were like family. They still called Claire Teeny.

Even when they came for some other reason, they ended up having their cards read. Claire liked Violet and Poppy, especially Poppy. Violet was from West Virginia, and there were things about her that reminded Claire of Hugh's family. Violet's husband drank and was sick and did not work. Violet had worked at the sewing factory for years. Sometimes she made small things for Claire.

Claire liked to watch the readings. Later, after Violet and Poppy left, she asked Eleanor to teach her. Eleanor said no.

She asked Eleanor to read her cards.

"You're too young," Eleanor said.

Claire had heard of other card readers but never met one. Storefront windows glowed neon: "Psychic Reader." Eleanor said those women were fake. Claire did not know of any books that explained cards. If Eleanor would not teach her, she would have to teach herself.

She had a Ouija board that she and her friends used. Claire thought it was fake. She could always tell when someone was pushing the planchette. The other girls acted frightened and told ghost stories.

She did not know if she had ever seen a ghost.

She knew the cards worked. People who came to Eleanor always returned, telling how right she had been. After that, Claire began to memorize the readings—watched the shuffling and cuts, learned the suits: Kings, Queens, Jacks for people, certain numbers for children or travel. She remembered everything.

Once she asked if some people's cards were easier to read than others.

"Yes," Eleanor said. She paused. "With Poppy I hardly need the cards. I can read her mind. With some people I can only see what the cards tell me."

Claire stored that away.

Bucky worked on his bright red MG in front of the house. The running boards shone. The wire wheels caught the light. The hood was long and narrow. He said it was a classic.

When he lowered the cloth top, he sometimes took Claire for short rides. The wind blew her hair across her eyes.

He had Ray's mechanical talent. Unlike Ray, he read thick paperbacks with small print and said little. Once he told Claire that a friend in the Army had walked into a plane propeller. After that he did not mention the Army again.

He had finished his time with the Special Forces and had joined the Marines. He would be leaving again soon and was staying with Eleanor, Hugh, and Claire. His room was on the third floor across the hall from Mrs. Cooper and Audrey. The doors had locks and keys.

Audrey had finished high school and worked as a receptionist in a law office. On Saturdays she and Claire walked to the stores up on Harford Road. Audrey bought shampoo and bubble bath. Claire bought records.

One Saturday, Claire's hair was set in curlers. It would take hours to dry. She planned to leave them in until the last minute. Audrey said to put a scarf over them. Claire said no. Audrey said women did it all the time. Nobody important would see her. Claire tied one of Eleanor's scarves over the curlers.

GC Murphy sold everything on Audrey's list. They kept the records near a stairway that came up from the basement by the front door.

There was a boy at school Claire watched more than the others. He carried a guitar case. As Claire headed toward the records, the boy came up the stairs, carrying the case. Long hair. Jeans. Beatle boots. Claire held her breath. She wasn't even sure he knew her name.

He saw her.

"Hi Claire," he said.

"Hi," she said.

They passed without stopping.

All weekend she thought about it. Certain he must think she was hideous. On Monday he sat behind her in class. Nothing was different.

Halfway through the period, he tapped her shoulder and passed a folded note. Her stomach lifted as she opened it.

He wanted to meet a blonde girl he could see with her gym class, out the window. Claire knew the girl from Home Ec., but they were not friends.

She wrote "yes" and passed the note back.

At home things were changing.

Audrey talked more to Bucky.

One evening Claire left her room and went down the hall to the bathroom. Audrey and Bucky were in the living room kissing. Claire walked past as if she had not seen them.

Later Eleanor mentioned Bucky and Audrey going out together.

Claire said nothing.

After a few weeks Bucky went to the Marine base at Parris Island.

Billy came to the apartment for the first time in his uniform. He was a private first class in the infantry. Audrey blushed when she met him. He stayed in the room where Bucky had stayed before.

Two days later Claire saw them in the living room kissing the way Audrey had kissed Bucky.

Claire asked Eleanor about it.

Eleanor shook her head.

"Billy doesn't really care about that girl," she said. "He just wanted to take her away from Bucky."

Since they had moved to Northeast Baltimore, Eleanor returned to her habit of joining the nearest Protestant church. The Methodist church stood half a block from the apartment, a brick building with a white steeple.

Inside, it was plain. At St. Boniface on Harford Road the crosses held a figure of Jesus. Here the cross was smooth brass. The priest at St. Boniface wore a cassock. The Methodist minister wore a suit. No matter the neighborhood, most of Claire's friends were Catholic. That seemed normal. Sometimes she went with them—their churches were beautiful, more to watch. Usually, she went with Eleanor to the Methodist church.

The year of the New York World's Fair, the Methodist church filled a chartered bus and drove north before daylight. The fair said it showed the future.

She saw a telephone with a screen where a person's face appeared while they spoke. There was a train that ran on a single rail above the ground. In one building people stepped onto a moving walkway and did not have to walk at all. One ride carried them in small cars through long dim rooms. Rows of dolls stood behind low fences, each dressed in the clothes of a different country. They rocked and turned their heads and sang in thin voices while the cars drifted past. Claire watched until the last row disappeared into the dark. After the Fair, the singing dolls went to Disneyland's "Small World."

Not long after the trip, Eleanor said she had news about Bucky. He'd had some trouble in the Marines and was in a mental hospital out in the county. They would go to see him.

The bus ride took most of the morning.

The hospital stood above a wide lawn that sloped toward the water. Before they went inside Eleanor and Claire sat on the grass. Eleanor said people must not hear about this. It would follow him. It would follow all of them. She said it would go on his record. She said the doctors wanted to give Bucky electroshock treatments. She called him schizophrenic. When Claire asked what that meant, Eleanor said he heard voices that were not there.

Claire asked about the treatments. Eleanor said they would send electricity through his head to quiet his mind. Claire looked out at the water. It did not sound right. Eleanor said she had to sign permission papers. The doctors told her that if she signed, Bucky might come home, but if she did not sign he would stay there the rest of his life. They said it was the only sensible course.

Claire wanted Eleanor to refuse and take him away, but Eleanor said there was no choice.

Then they went inside. There were guards and locked doors and men who shuffled along the hall with glassy eyes. Claire did not want Bucky in a place like this.

Claire couldn't stop coughing again.

The doctor's office was down the block. Uphill from the house was the church. Downhill was the doctor. Eleanor took her in without calling first. The doctor knew them. Claire was there often.

Bronchitis again. Chronic bronchitis, he said. Antibiotics. Vaporizer. Stay inside. No school for a few days.

He talked about smoking. One of his lungs had been removed because of cancer. He still smoked. Eleanor smoked. Hugh smoked. Claire tried a cigarette once. It was hot and bitter and made her feel sick. She stopped before the third drag and never tried again.

Eighth grade felt different.

She was back at Franklin Junior High and saw the same students she had met at the end of seventh grade. Everyone had grown taller. She was no longer the smallest in the class. She stood above many of the girls and a few of the boys.

All the girls wore bras now. Some of the boys' voices cracked and turned froggy when they spoke. The children from seventh grade had disappeared. No one looked young anymore.

Claire watched to see where she fit.

She dressed carefully and noticed which girls wore clothes like hers. She studied the boys who looked like the musicians on the record covers she bought.

At recess they stood in a circle on the blacktop and talked. One of the girls asked, "Are you a Mod or a Rocker?" Each of them answered in turn. Claire said she wasn't sure.

The girl looked her up and down and smiled. "You're a Mod. Look at you."

Claire understood it was approval. After that she said she was persuaded Eleanor to buy her shoes that came from England. She refused to wear corrective shoes again. Eleanor allowed it so long as the shoes passed Eleanor's test of practicality.

Claire studied fashion magazines to see how to apply makeup. She would not use the liquid base and powder Eleanor recommended to hide her pale skin and the freckles across her nose. Instead, she wore white lipstick and black eyeliner. She drew lines beneath her eyes to imitate extra lashes, like Twiggy.

She wore textured stockings, often white or a color that did not match her legs. She kept track of the newest styles. The cool students treated her as one of them. Others laughed because they had never seen anyone dressed that way. She did not mind.

She stopped raising her hand in class.

If a lesson bored her, she filled her notebook with drawings and kept a book open in front of her as if she were reading. She never did homework assignments. She decided she did not care about grades.

At home Hugh yelled at her more often and beat her more often. Once, when he was very drunk and shouting, he hit her and she hit back. She had never done that before. Her nails caught his neck. He looked surprised. She ran to her room and slammed the door. She was afraid he might follow. He did not. He fell asleep and forgot.

When he woke, he asked Eleanor how he had gotten the scratches. Claire remembered that.

Sometimes he chased her down the hallway with his belt. Sometimes he threw his boots. She locked herself in the bathroom until he went away. Eleanor quieted him until he passed out, but she did not stop the fights.

At the second-floor landing there was a newel post with a loose top. Eleanor said someone would break their neck someday and told Hugh to fix it. He never did.

One night he chased Claire with the belt again. Instead of running to the bathroom, she ran down the stairs. She knew he would follow. She knew he would grab the loose post. She did not touch it when she passed. He did. The post shifted in his hand and he fell down the stairs.

He was not badly hurt. He slept afterward, the way he always did. After that, he avoided starting more arguments with Claire.

After school, Claire met Cynthia and Minette and walked part of the way home with them. Cynthia lived farther up Harford Road, on a side street across from where Minette lived.

They met Dean along the way. He was in seventh grade but tall enough to pass for older. He noticed the clothes Claire had made herself, the little details in the finishing, and she liked that. He walked with them as far as his house.

Each day he kissed one of them on the lips while the other two waved and kept walking. The turns came evenly. Sometimes they went inside. His grandmother sat in the living room, watching TV, hardly looking up. Two girls stayed with her while the third went downstairs with Dean to the basement playroom. They sat on the sofa and kissed.

When it was Claire's turn, he tried to slip his hand under her shirt. She said no. He argued, mentioned that Minette had let him, and talked about "doing it."

Claire sat up straight. "If I said yes, you wouldn't even know what to do. You just want to be told yes." He agreed at once. She had expected an argument. They went back upstairs, where Batman played on the TV. Cartoon words floated over the live action: POW! BOOM! WHAMM!

The basement ritual stopped after that. The four still hung out near his house after school. Friends. They never talked about it at school. He was a seventh grader. Below them.

The holidays came. Claire asked Eleanor if they could have a traditional Thanksgiving. Eleanor roasted a small turkey with bread stuffing. She also roasted a duck for Hugh and made mashed potatoes, sweet potatoes, sauerkraut, and green beans. Pumpkin pie arrived with their weekly order from Rice's bakery, which also brought sliced bread and Hugh's favorite Vienna bread. Occasionally they got a Louisiana ring cake or a box of doughnuts. Eleanor's account helped keep them fed from paycheck to paycheck.

They ate at the Formica and chrome kitchen table. Claire tried to feel festive, but she noticed that in every picture she had seen of Thanksgiving, the families were larger, seated in dining rooms. Eleanor said,

"We are going to have a lot of leftovers."

Christmas was quiet, but bright. They got a big tree for the living room. Eleanor decorated it with glass ornaments they had kept for years, added icicles slowly, a few at a time, and hung candy canes. Their lights were all different colors on a single string. Boxes wrapped in paper and ribbon sat underneath.

Claire opened a box and found the jacket she had asked for. Soft dark suede, with covered leather buttons. Other girls in her class already had one, and this was at the top of her list. Another box held three yards of fabric. Eleanor said she had gotten fabric once for Christmas as a child, and it had been the best present she ever received. Claire agreed it was a pretty great gift.

New Year's Eve arrived. Eleanor and Hugh seemed excited. Eleanor told Hugh, "You can be the dark-haired man this year." He agreed. They had both grown up with a tradition: a dark-haired man would knock on a neighbor's door just after midnight, be the first person in the household, and bring luck for the year. A small bottle of whiskey, a silver coin, or a box of salt. Hugh was perfect for it.

All three stayed up until midnight. "Happy New Year!" they said, and Hugh went off to knock on a few doors. Claire could hear laughter drifting from the street as she fell asleep.

"Sit in the hall. You can't be in this class if you won't pay attention."

Eighth-grade algebra was the worst class. Math had always been the worst. Until third grade Claire wrote her numbers backwards, a three turned the wrong way like an E. She had never learned the multiplication tables. Algebra looked like code. Back in fourth grade she thought you might solve it by turning numbers into letters and spelling words.

By eighth grade, she had stopped trying. The teacher had a sharp voice and looked at Claire as if she had already made up her mind.

She did not learn any math sitting alone in the hall. She drew instead. The swirly lines of her doodles took her to another place. She practiced drawing the things around her, tiny pen drawings in the margins of her papers.

At home she worked on her clothes and her record collection, learning which styles suited her and which songs she wanted to hear again and again. She and Hugh stayed out of each other's way.

She wanted her ears pierced. Eleanor said no. Claire kept asking why. The talk about infection and pain did not make sense. Finally, Eleanor turned on her.

"Only gypsies and whores have pierced ears."

Claire knew that wasn't true. She dropped it for now.

She did not play piano anymore. Uncle Leroy brought her an acoustic guitar. She liked the sound, but the strings hurt her fingers. Turning piano notes into guitar notes in her head made her tired. She did not think she wanted to be a guitar player.

On Saturdays she sometimes went to Cynthia's house on a side street. Cynthia liked the same music and had persuaded her parents to let her go to a concert with Claire. It was the first for both of them. For weeks they planned what to wear, changing their minds until the last day, when each chose a favorite mod skirt and matching jacket.

Outside the Civic Center the crowd pressed in from all sides. Policemen on horses moved through it, pushing people back. One horse came close to Claire. Its head dipped and rose. Foam fell from its mouth into her hair. She stood still for a moment, then took Cynthia's hand and moved toward the entrance.

They went inside. Their seats were close to the stage, but up on the mezzanine.

Bo Diddley played first. Then the Rolling Stones came out.

Claire and Cynthia left their seats and sat on the floor, leaning through the guard rail toward the stage. No one stopped them.

Claire watched Brian Jones's egg-shaped guitar. Keith Richards looked like someone she might have known. Mick Jagger looked a little ugly and completely right at the same time.

Cynthia said she would see the Beatles when they came to town.

Another day, Cynthia showed her how to steal from Read's drugstore. Everyone took makeup, Cynthia said. They went in together and came out with things they had not paid for.

Claire did not like the feeling and never did it again. Cynthia kept doing it.

Cynthia borrowed clothes from Claire. Claire always had to ask for them back, and they always came back dirty. One dress Claire had made and designed herself. Cynthia would not return it even when Claire asked. Eventually, Claire stopped asking, or even talking to Cynthia at all.

One day they passed in the school hallway. Cynthia was wearing the dress. Navy blue with tiny white dots and a white collar and cuffs. There was a stain on one cuff.

Cynthia was talking as she walked and did not see Claire.

Claire was walking with Laurie and Denise. She pretended not to notice Cynthia or the dress.

Thief, she thought.

Looking at her report card, Claire thought maybe refusing basketball hadn't been such a great idea. She had flunked algebra and gym.

Gym was as bad as math. Everybody undressing, the showers, the noise. Especially when Mrs. Fowler was in the locker room. Bermuda shorts, knobby knees, whistle on a chain, man's haircut.

In elementary school phys ed had been fun. Volleyball, balance beam, rope climbing. Team sports were not. The rules—how many times to bounce, when to jump—too much. The locker room was chaos, no privacy. She wrote excuse notes to the teacher and signed Eleanor's name. When she had to be there, she refused to play.

Now, summer school so she wouldn't be left back in eighth grade. Eleanor and Hugh were disappointed. Claire thought they were unfair. They didn't understand.

All the summer school students from all over Baltimore went to Poly on North Avenue. Buses came from everywhere. She recognized a few kids. One boy from elementary school said, loud, "Claire Young? I never thought you'd have to go to summer school!" Another boy from the other side of town asked for her phone number. He called once. It was too far to visit. They never talked again.

Claire learned enough to pass. Ninth grade next.

That summer Billy married Audrey from downstairs at the Methodist church on the corner. The wedding was small. Her cousin stood as maid of honor, his friend as best man. Bucky, recently released from the hospital, was in the wedding party. Claire thought the wedding looked sparse, like the church.

When she wasn't in school Claire wore her newest outfits and walked up to the Harford Road commercial strip. She stopped in the kitchen to say she was going. Sometimes they made her change.

Eleanor said the skirt was too short or the pants too tight. Today it was the jeans. Claire knew the jeans fit right. She didn't move.

"Your pants make you look like you have a big ass," Eleanor said. "You were always too skinny," Eleanor added. "Now, you're getting broad in the beam."

Hugh leaned against the counter. "Upper frontal architecture," he said quietly. Claire knew that meant her sweater was too tight. Eleanor shot him a look. Claire wrinkled her nose. Another stupid hillbilly comment.

She left the kitchen wearing tight black jeans and a white sleeveless sweater, wondering if her hips were too big.

Out on Harford Road boys in a car honked and yelled something she didn't understand. Her stomach tightened. She froze for a second, then kept walking.

The Arcade movie theater sat near the end of a long hall lined with shops. She would never go to a movie by herself, but she liked looking in the shop windows. The jewelry store was her favorite. Sometimes a glint would catch her eye and she would stop.

She wanted the silver and enamel snake ring that wrapped around the finger. She didn't have the money, and thought girls were not supposed to buy rings for themselves.

She stood a moment longer and then walked on.

PART FOUR

Claire had been in the same building since the end of seventh grade.
Now she was in ninth. The lockers were no longer new; the floors held the
same dull shine. The same teachers in the hallway standing like islands as
the river of students passed by. It was the longest she had stayed anywhere.
She chose a seat near the back. In the front rows you had to look interested. From the back she could see everyone—the girls smoothing their
skirts, the boys sitting straighter when a teacher passed. She drew in her
notebook while the lessons went on. Faces. Eyes. The curve of a sleeve.
A hand on a desk. The hands were hard to draw.

Sometimes a question floated back to her. If she knew it, she raised
her hand and answered, as if she had been listening all along. She did not
do homework. The test scores were enough.

Math was different. The numbers would not line up for her, and the
teacher seemed to take that personally. The room felt smaller.

In art class, she stopped drawing in the margins and worked on
what was assigned. She was never quite satisfied with what she drew but
kept trying.

She got sick again. Strep throat and then something the doctor
called Quinsy. Her throat hurt more than ever. She could barely open her
mouth. More antibiotics. More time off school.

At night she watched *Mission: Impossible* with Eleanor and Hugh—
the spark, the sound of bongo drums and flute, the fuse burning down.
In her room she watched *Star Trek* and *That Girl* alone, the blue light
flickering against the dresser. There was a world somewhere beyond the
ceiling of her room. Songs about change, rebellion, and wandering spilled
out of the radio. The news showed helicopters lifting off, crowds in the
streets, men shouting into microphones. Cities she had only heard the
names of flashed on screens. It seemed as if something was happening
without her.

There were protests. She knew Eleanor would never allow her to
stand in a crowd like that, and her friends had no interest in marching
anywhere. So she stayed in her room and played her records. She lifted
each album from its sleeve and studied the covers—the clothes, the faces,

the way they stood. She held them as if they might explain something.

Sometimes she and Eleanor went to the movies.

A few years earlier they had gone downtown to the Mayfair to see *Mary Poppins.* They went in the afternoon. When they came out, lights were twinkling in the dark. The night felt wide open. Claire always remembered that feeling.

They saw *The Sound of Music.* Afterward, Claire liked the way Maria unsettled the house. The whistle at the window. The curtains cut down and stitched into play clothes. The children running where they weren't supposed to run. Eleanor liked that Maria found true love.

They both liked the part where the family fooled the Nazis and escaped.

The girls stood in a loose circle at the edge of the church hall, backs to a row of metal folding chairs, watching the line of boys across the room pretend not to watch them. The CYO dances pulled in everyone—Catholic, Protestant, whomever had a dollar and a ride. A local band played every Saturday night. On the better nights there was a battle of the bands, amps humming, singers wailing and growling, the drums hitting clean and deep, right through Claire's ribs.

Claire knew some of the boys onstage from school. Some were older. They played covers mostly, with one or two original songs slipped in between. She wasn't interested in the boys along the wall. They looked idle, waiting. The boys on stage were all focus. Every note, every gesture aimed at the crowd.

She danced with her friends in a tight pack, the way girls did then—arms up, hair swinging, no one singled out. If a boy asked, she would give him one fast song. Not a slow one. Slow dancing meant hands at her waist, breath near her ear. That was for someone chosen. She didn't want practice hands on her.

They studied one another's dresses, the fall of a hem, the shape of eyeliner. What you wore mattered. Some weeks Claire remade an old blouse or cut apart a skirt and brought it back altered, just to see their faces when she walked in. She liked the moment before anyone spoke.

At home, Eleanor stood in the kitchen light and pointed out the hump in Claire's nose, the hem that was too short, the lipstick too pale. Claire said, "Do you even think I'm pretty?"

Eleanor blinked once, as if considering it. "You have nice eyebrows." Claire read fashion magazines the way other girls studied for tests. She searched for a face among the models' that looked like hers. There were not many brunettes. Colleen Corby had pale skin, dark hair, and a young face. She was mildly inspiring. Twiggy was everywhere, but Claire preferred Peggy Moffitt—the sharp liner, the black and white precisely painted lines, the sculpted, shining cut. Moffitt had modeled the topless bathing suit designed by Rudi Gernreich. Claire would never wear that suit. She copied the eyeliner instead. She thickened her bangs. She bought false eyelashes and learned to set them straight. Eleanor puckered her mouth but did not forbid it.

In the back pages of *Seventeen* she found an advertisement for the Fashion Institute of Technology in New York. The ad listed careers: designer, illustrator, buyer. She imagined an old loft space with tall factory windows and a dressmaker's mannequin standing in the light. When she told Eleanor, Eleanor said, "Maybe you could be a fashion buyer for a department store." Claire tried the idea on, turned it slightly, made it fit.

If buyer meant New York, she could begin there.

First, she had to finish high school.

In October there was the Fall Family Frolic. Some boys played in their bands. Some kids played music alone, read poems, or did magic. In Home Ec., Mrs. Lacey picked girls to model what they'd made. Claire was picked for her skirt. Brown and black herringbone wool. A-line. Mini. She liked the way it swung when she walked.

Ninth grade was louder socially and narrower in every other way. Teachers measured skirt lengths, checked to see if boys' hair was longer than the tops of their collars and made students spit out their gum. In Mrs. White's typing class, she kept her eyes above the keys and tapped out forty-five words per minute—the minimum to pass. Eleanor had placed her in the Business/College Prep track.

French sat on the page in neat columns; she liked reading it but hated saying it aloud, couldn't roll her r's. Math stayed closed behind the teacher's glare.

She moved between classes, noticing who got singled out and who could slip by. A world beyond school was there, waiting. She would have to find her own rhythm and then push past it.

Her old enemies, math and gym, were on the report card again. Summer school. Six weeks at Poly with the other Baltimore kids who had failed one or two subjects. The alternative was another year of junior high: not an option.

She dressed carefully the first morning. The baby-doll dress with the puffed sleeves and scooped neckline. The seam drew tight just under her bust and fell straight from there. In the full-length mirror she turned once. The dresses she made herself knew where to hold and where to let go.

The class was what she expected. If you came, you passed.

The building had no air conditioning. The room stayed hot. A thin line of sweat slid down the neck of the boy in front of her and disappeared into his collar. She hoped her after-bath splash and powder would hold.

She spun the glass birthstone ring on her right hand with her thumb. It was supposed to be an emerald. It wasn't. The gold was real. It had been her father Hugh's birthday gift, bought after she told him she'd seen it in a jewelry store and said, "My daddy will be in to buy it for me."

The first weeks passed quickly. She rode the bus home and sometimes played badminton with Betty, the birdie arcing over the net until the light thinned. On hotter days they used the pool Hugh and Eleanor had put up in the backyard. Three feet deep and ten feet across. Big enough to cool off. Betty would arrive with two colored metal glasses of iced tea and climb in.

It was a lazy summer. Some kids found jobs and brought home pay envelopes. Summer school excused Claire from that. She had afternoons.

On the last day of the last week, she crossed North Avenue toward the bus. The light lay flat on the pavement bleaching everything out. Kids from everywhere. Some she knew. Some she didn't. She heard a voice behind her and turned.

Steve from ninth grade stood there with a boy a little older than she was and a little taller. The red of the boy's hair looked like fire in the glare. "Claire, my friend wants to meet you. This is Jimmy Marino."

He said hello without hesitation. They climbed the bus steps together. He was noticeable because of his red hair. Not her usual type. She tended toward dark hair, quiet faces, something withheld. He was only about five-eight but solid through the shoulders, lean and compact. Wavy red hair with lighter streaks, bright green eyes that squinted, a big Roman nose, a generous mouth quick to smile. Acne along the jaw and temples. He came up the bus steps easy, one hand on the rail, glancing down the aisle like someone who could take the world as it came.

The bus moved up Harford Road and they exchanged the basics. At Franklin Avenue she stepped down. He stayed on toward Mercer Avenue, her phone number folded in his pocket.

At home she went to her room and put on a record. She lay back and listed what she knew. Jeans. Jack Purcell fish-head sneakers. A short-sleeved tattersall shirt. Thick red hair, lighter at the ends. Taller than she. Maybe a year older. Green eyes that narrowed when he laughed. A wide mouth. Acne. He played drums.

Claire was drying dishes for Eleanor when the phone rang. She wiped her
hands on the towel and reached for the wall receiver. "Hello."
It was Jimmy Marino. He asked if she would go with him to the carnival
at Double Rock Park in Parkville on Friday night. She held the cord in
her fingers and listened while he explained about the rides and meeting at
the bus stop. She hesitated. She did not want to tell him she had to ask.
She said yes.

After she hung up, she went back to the sink. "Can I go to a carnival
Friday?"

Eleanor kept her hands in the suds. "Where?"

"Double Rock."

"With who?"

"A boy I met. Jimmy Marino. We'd take the bus."

Now Eleanor turned. The questions came steadily. Where does he
live? How old is he? What school? What do his parents do?

"He lives on Mercer Avenue. He's a year older than me." The rest she
did not know. Color moved into her face.

"Marino," Eleanor said. "Italian."

"He has red hair," Claire said.

"There are blond Italians. It depends what part of Italy his family is from."

Eleanor rinsed a glass and set it upside down on the towel.

Claire wanted to go to her room and lie on her bed and think.
Friday she laid out clothes across the bed. Navy blue culottes. Ring-toe
sandals. Sleeveless shell. She poured Mr. Bubble into running water,
watched the foam rise, fitted the shower cap hours before leaving.

When it was time, Eleanor stood in the doorway. "Be good.
Have fun. Home before nine. Make sure he doesn't let you walk alone."

Claire nodded, relieved that Eleanor hadn't asked to meet him.
Jimmy's smile made her see he was glad to see her. Her first real date. She
wanted to make a good impression.

They stepped onto the bus. Jimmy put in both fares. She noticed
that there weren't many people on the bus. He talked easily about playing
drums, saying words like paradiddle and fatback. He said he had been in a

band before and was going to get another one soon. He laughed, saying his father yelled at him for tapping beats in his head. Imitating his father, he used a loud, gruff voice:

"Tap, tap, tap! What's the matter with you?!"

They laughed. She was glad she didn't have to talk much.

They got off the bus and walked toward the park. She could see the rides from a distance. The Ferris wheel was stopped with people sitting in a swinging seat on the top. They were laughing and looking down. Claire noticed the Tilt-a-Whirl. One of her favorites, though she didn't say so.

Jimmy grabbed her hand and headed for the Midway. The air smelled like popcorn, cotton candy, and beer. The colored lights made everything feel like a dream. He played a shooting game to win stuffed animal prizes but came away empty handed. She looked at his arms. Lean and strong, with big, thick hands.

He seemed to like her watching. "My father says I have bricklayer's hands."

They mostly walked around the carnival, holding hands, looking at each booth. She had never walked around holding hands with a boy before and wondered how they looked together.

Jimmy didn't seem the same as he did on the bus. At first she thought maybe he was nervous like she was. By the time they were walking back toward Harford Road, she noticed he was staggering a little. At the bus stop, he didn't want to wait. "Let's walk until we see the bus coming." Her feet hurt from so much walking, but she went along. He wavered, then straightened and walked deliberately.

A knot formed in her stomach. She recognized it from seeing Hugh try to act sober. This was different, but the same. She didn't smell alcohol, but his eyes looked a little odd, off track somehow.

By the time they reached her front yard, she felt like she had been through some ordeal, though she wasn't sure what. He kissed her. She liked it more than she expected.

"I'll talk to you soon."

She went directly to her room and turned on the radio. The Mamas and Papas' voices came out of the speaker.

She sat on the bed and bit her nails.

79 Saints

It was Monday afternoon. Her parents were at work, the house quiet when Jimmy appeared.

"Hi…what are you doing here?" She led him to the living room. He stayed standing, shoulders tense. For a second she just looked at him. Then he spoke.

"You know the tunnels over by Belair Road?"

Claire nodded. She knew the concrete caves were there. Wide enough to swallow a car. Black water ran through after rain.

"I was on my way back from there—that's where we hang out. Me and my friends. They're great guys. They joke with me about being a red-headed Wop." Claire didn't see the joke.

"When they see me, they say, 'I'd rather be dead than red in the head.' And I say, 'I'd rather be red than dead in the head!'" His laugh faded quickly.

He picked at a loose thread on the cushion.

"What do you do there?" she asked.

"We sniff glue sometimes. Tester's airplane glue. The kind in the silver tube. Or Carbona." Claire tilted her head. She didn't know what he was talking about.

"It's a carpet cleaner."

She froze. He didn't look away. He kept talking.

"You put it in a bag. Roll the top down. Put it over your face. Huff it."

She noticed a smear of dried glue on his jacket.

The room smelled faintly of Pledge.

"One of the guys, Pete, he's got a gun. He's a badass." He shrugged.

"Sometimes he's got pills too. White crosses. Dilaudid."

"Do you take them?"

"Sometimes I do sets."

She looked at him.

"Uppers and downers together," he said. "Feels good."

He said it like he was describing a radio station.

"We call ourselves The Saints." He smirked once, without humor.

He looked at her then, quick, measuring. Her expression must have said enough.

"I want to stop huffin'," he said. "I can stop."

Claire didn't speak. Her lips pressed together. Her eyebrows lifted.

"If you keep goin' with me," he said. "I'll quit. Swear to God."

He rubbed his hands together, then held them still between his knees.

"It's just somethin' to do," he said. "If you don't like it, I can stop."

The apartment was very clean. The doilies lay flat. Hugh's ashtray faced forward.

Jimmy waited.

She looked at his hands. The nails were rimmed dark. A faint sweet smell clung to him that did not belong in the living room.

Hugh's ashtray sat square on its doily.

"I don't want you sniffing glue."

"Okay." He said.

"I'm making chicken," Jimmy said.

"You make dinner for your family?"

"Yeah. I put spices on it and stick it in the oven for an hour."

"What kind of spices?"

"Salt, pepper, cinnamon, crushed red pepper, oregano."

The chicken lay pale on a metal tray. Eleanor's food came plain—salt, if she was feeling reckless. Claire pictured putting cinnamon on meat in her mother's kitchen and the look that would follow.

She stepped back from him and the bird. "Cinnamon? On chicken? That's weird."

He shrugged. "It can work. I try stuff."

She tried to imagine a house where you could try stuff with cooking.

It was the first time she'd been inside Jimmy's house. No voices. No television. No one calling from another room.

"When do your parents get home?"

"Later. My grandmother's here, but she's sleeping. My sister Gina'll be back soon."

Gina arrived in a rush of dark hair and quick steps. She was short, compact, with sharp Italian eyes and a friendly face. She didn't resemble Jimmy much.

Gina had gone to Catholic school for junior high and planned to go to Eastern like her sisters. She and Claire were the same age, birthdays only days apart. She had a boyfriend from up near St. Boniface. He was coming over.

Jimmy took Claire to the basement. It was half-finished, cool, smelling faintly of concrete and laundry soap. A sofa sagged along one wall. A single chair with a low back and a small pillow on the seat behind his drum kit. He sat down and tapped out a beat, then another. The beats got louder as he went from using brushes to sticks and mallets, showing her the different tools. The sound filled the room, rose up through her ribs. She stood close enough to feel it in her chest, in her teeth. It was loud and clean and unapologetic.

When he stopped, the quiet felt sudden.

They sat on the couch. They kissed. His hands were careful at first, then less so. The basement felt separate from the house above it.

"Let's go upstairs," she said.

His grandmother was awake now, folded into a large armchair, a teacup balanced in her hand. The drums must have stirred her, though she said nothing. She was so small she seemed arranged there. A miniature French poodle sat on her lap, white fur, stained brown around the mouth.

"This is Fifi," the grandmother said. "Kathleen's dog. The stains are from coffee."

Jimmy laughed. Claire did, too.

He bent and kissed the old woman's cheek. "Grandma Bridget, this is Claire."

"Hello, Claire. Will you stay for dinner?"

"No, thank you. I have to be home."

Gina's boyfriend, Tony, knocked on the door. Gina flew from her bedroom and out the door in one motion.

Jimmy told his grandmother what time to take the chicken out of the oven in case he wasn't back.

They walked the few blocks toward Claire's house.

He called the woman in the chair his little grandmother. "She's eighty-five. She calls cars machines." "She'll say, 'Are we walking or taking the machine?'" "Her name's Bridget Kelley," he said. "Irish to the bone. My mother's mother."

"My Italian grandmother, Mama Dear, lives up the street. She makes food and brings it over a few times a week. She don't speak English."

Claire said she liked Gina.

"She's the youngest," he said. "I'm second youngest and my sister Sandy is older. Josie is the oldest. My brother Robert was in the Army." He paused. Claire said, "My brother Bucky was in the Army too. My brother Billy still is." There was a second of silence as each of them went into their own thoughts.

"Gina hasn't been with Tony that long," Jimmy said. "He's a real badass." Claire nodded.

Jimmy said he wanted Claire to come for dinner sometime, meet everyone. "Just be prepared."

166

"For what?"

"My dad used to box. 'Ironfist Vinny.' Now he works for Mama Dear's construction company."

"Your grandmother owns a construction company?"

"'Third husband did. He left it to her."

"My dad and my uncles all work for her."

"And your mother?" Claire asked.

"She's where I got the red hair."

They passed peaked roofs, wide bungalows, lawns worn in the same places year after year. The neighborhood looked settled into itself. People had stayed.

Jimmy had stayed.

Claire could not remember ever knowing anyone so entirely unself-conscious.

Claire hadn't talked to Cynthia in months.

One afternoon she appeared at the curb on the back of a Yamaha 90, arms looped around a boy who lived a few streets over. The engine buzzed high and thin. Cynthia's hair lifted in the exhaust. She waited a second before looking toward the house.

Eleanor noticed. "Everywhere that girl goes, trouble goes with her."

The boy cut the engine. The quiet dropped hard around them. Claire stepped off the porch and walked closer. The bike looked smaller up close but heavier—metal, cables, heat ticking from the engine. She liked the smell of gasoline.

He took Claire once around the block, while Cynthia waited. The vibration ran straight through her spine. The houses softened at the edges. When they stopped, she didn't want to get off.

"Can I try?" she said.

"Just down the block."

She was too young for a license but that didn't seem to matter. He explained the brakes, front and back.

"Remember, front brakes are on the handlebars, for back brakes, use the pedal."

She nodded.

The bike lurched, then steadied. She moved forward, surprised at the clean pull of it, at the way the street opened ahead. She got maybe twenty feet. The front brake caught hard. She hadn't touched the pedal for the back brakes.

Everything jerked to a halt.

She went forward. The bike didn't. She screamed. Her face hit the curb. For a moment, nothing hurt. Only a bright, blank sound filled her head.

Eleanor came running.

Claire was sitting up when she reached her. Blood slid from her lip onto her chin. Gravel stuck to her palms. One side of her face was already swelling.

At the emergency room they said her cheekbone was cracked. No displacement. It would heal on its own. Claire, who'd crashed without a helmet, also had a concussion.

A black eye bloomed, dark and theatrical. A hard knot rose along her cheek and stayed there through the end of summer, into the first weeks of tenth grade. She could feel it when she washed her face. A ridge under the skin.

People asked what happened.

"I was driving a motorcycle," she said.

She didn't add that it had only been twenty feet.

She let them picture the rest.

The air had been thick all afternoon, and the sky broke open while Claire and Jimmy were walking. She took her sandals off and carried them, letting the rain soak her clothes and hair. Jimmy kept his shoes on. They gave in to the drenching and walked down the middle of the street. Water ran down their faces and they didn't wipe it away. She spun once and nearly slipped. They both laughed.

Thunder cracked overhead. Lightning lit the clouds. Claire jumped and caught his arm. They laughed again.

Then the rain stopped as suddenly as it had started. Water dripped from their clothes and hair. They kept walking, soaked through.

When they got to Claire's house, she invited him in to dry off. Eleanor was home.

"Mom, this is Jimmy."

Eleanor brought towels from the bathroom, a little flustered, laughing once for no reason as she handed them over. Jimmy tried to keep the water from dripping on the kitchen floor.

"Hi, Jimmy. It's nice to meet you," Eleanor said, smiling at him the way she smiled at puppies and kittens.

"Happy to meet you, Mrs. Young." He nodded. "But I better get home."

Claire walked him to the door.

When she came back to the kitchen Eleanor said, "He seems like a nice boy."

Claire paused. Eleanor was usually so critical.

"Oh, he is," she said, and went to her room to change into dry clothes.

Claire came back. Eleanor was in the living room.

"Where were you two?"

"At his house. Watching TV."

"Anyone else there?"

"His sister Gina. Her boyfriend Tony. And his grandmother—she's always home."

They really had been watching TV. Gina on Tony's lap, arms wrapped around him. He leaned back, taking up the overstuffed chair, shoulders wide. Claire had seen him on the corner across from St. Boniface, with the other older boys who always hung out there. He had looked at her, shifting his gaze, and she edged back a little.

Eleanor cut in to Claire's thoughts.

"You should invite him over for dinner sometime."

"Um, OK. I'll let you know," Claire said.

She went to her room. Her wet clothes were draped over the chair where she had left them. The sandals she'd carried in her hand were still damp. She set them by the window and sat on the bed.

Her hair was still wet at the ends.

After a minute she pulled open the bottom drawer of her dresser and took out the old pair of jeans she had been saving along with a piece of fabric. She spread them flat on the bed. It was just enough.

On television Cher's pants flared wide at the bottom.

Claire folded the denim at the ankle and held the scissors there a moment.

Once she cut them they'd be ruined if it didn't work.

She cut.

Claire and her classmates were the second graduating class at the new Jones Falls High School. It was September 1966. They were sophomores, the class of '69.

Everything was new. The lockers still shone. The cafeteria was big, tiled floor and walls, long tables set end to end. Lunch ladies wore hairnets and rubber gloves. When people talked it echoed.

The school had an Olympic-sized swimming pool.

Claire had failed gym two years in a row. She hated team sports. She liked the water and she could swim. Maybe this year would be different.

The locker room had hair dryers bolted to the wall, rows of showers, metal lockers with working doors. The hair dryers sounded like airplane engines. The tile floor stayed wet all day.

The bathing suits belonged to the school. They were issued by size and the sizes were colors. The smallest girls wore aqua. Thin straps, flat chests, shoulder blades sharp under the cloth. Most girls wore red. Claire did too. She was relieved not to be the smallest or the biggest. Denise and Laurie from Harrison Jr. High wore red. The three of them stood together on the tile floor waiting for the whistle. Denise straightened the strap of her suit. The largest girls wore black. The towels were the same for everyone and too small for them. Some tried to hold them closed across the front. Some didn't bother.

No cover-ups were allowed.

Someone said the boys had to swim nude in their gym class. Everyone said that was the rule. The girls talked about it in the locker room, their voices low and shocked. Denise said it couldn't possibly be true. Laurie said her brother told her it was.

Claire pictured the boys standing at the edge of the pool waiting for the whistle. She hoped it wasn't true.

Claire liked swimming. She did not like swimming class.

She didn't like locker rooms or dressing with other people. She did not like being told when to get in the water and when to get out of it. School had a way of draining the pleasure out of things.

She went back to writing her own excuse notes.

Most were signed Eleanor Young. After a while the teachers saw so many of them, they stopped looking closely. Once, when Eleanor really signed one, the teacher held it up and said it looked forged.

The other classes did not hold her long, either.

In geography Miss Skinner walked between the desks and talked about rivers and trade winds while Claire drew in the margins of her notebook. Faces mostly. Eyes, mouths, hair. Sometimes dresses and coats.

"Miss Young," Miss Skinner said without looking down.

Claire closed the notebook.

The next day she drew again. Miss Skinner's shoes made soft sounds on the linoleum when she walked the rows. Sometimes she stopped behind Claire's chair for a moment before moving on.

Typing was still on her schedule. This year separated the real typists from the hunt-and-peck ones. There were a few boys in the room and about thirty girls. The room filled with the sound of keys striking and carriage bells ringing at the margin. Denise was already doing ninety words a minute the first week. The machine clattered when she got going. The teacher quickly moved her to the group allowed to use electric typewriters.

Claire could keep up well enough.

French was the same as before. She could read most of it. Speaking was another matter. Her R's refused to roll.

Home Ec. was worse.

Claire already knew how to cook. She had been doing it for years, mostly when Eleanor wasn't home.

She could lay a pattern on fabric, cut it out, and make a dress without help. She could shorten a hem, move a seam, add a ruffle.

Claire knew clothes.

The teacher could not sew. Claire could tell by the way she handled the fabric. When the class made their first garment the teacher stopped at Claire's desk and frowned at the zipper.

"How did you do that?"

Claire showed her.

Claire was furious when the teacher gave her a B instead of an A.

When she asked, the teacher said, "Attitude counts toward your grade."

There was no art class the first semester. Claire was disappointed.

At the end of the day, everyone poured out toward the buses. Rows of them waited with their engines running. Kids shouted across the pavement. Someone always had a radio playing. Boys shoved each other and yelled things at the girls climbing the steps. Claire got on her bus and took a seat by the window.

The bus filled slowly. A boy from her English class dropped into the seat across the aisle and immediately started arguing with someone two rows back about the Orioles. A girl Claire knew a little slid into the seat beside her and asked if she had the French homework written down. Claire told her what page it was on. More kids piled in. Someone in the back started singing something loud and stupid. A few people threw balled-up paper.

Claire watched it all move around her.

Outside the window more kids were still running for the buses.

After a few minutes the doors folded shut and the driver pulled out of the line.

Claire leaned her head against the window and watched the school slide away.

84   With the Band

The room was dark except for the stage.

Claire stood near the front, close enough to see the whole band if she shifted her eyes. Mostly, she watched Jimmy.

He was behind the drum kit, half hidden by the cymbals. The lights were bad—two colored bulbs with reflectors clipped to stands—so he showed mostly in outline. When he leaned forward the light caught the side of his face and the pale flash of the drumsticks.

One band had already played. Three more were on the bill. They all did cover songs. The same records everyone knew.

Joe stepped to the microphone.

"This next one—"

Claire watched Jimmy.

There was a second microphone set low, coming in on a boom from the side of the drums. She had noticed it earlier. Joe explained to the crowd: "Our drummer Jimmy is going to sing this one. Everybody get ready to party!"

Shout.

Claire looked at Jimmy.

He leaned toward the mic while his hands kept moving. Snare, hi-hat, snare. The beat came in first, steady and quick.

Then Jimmy's voice.

"Well—"

It came out rougher than Joe's. Lower.

Joe stepped back from the main microphone. He held two maracas in one hand and lifted them in the air, shaking them hard on the beat while he slapped his thigh with the other hand.

The bass player leaned toward his microphone.

Heyy heyy heyy.

Joe joined him.

Heyy heyy heyy!

The crowd knew the song. Couples moved closer together on the floor. Girls in skirts bent their knees and laughed when Jimmy started singing "a little bit lower now." The room warmed and thickened with motion.

Claire didn't dance.

She stood still, watching.

Jimmy leaned toward the microphone again, singing while he played. His shoulders moved with the beat. The cymbal flashed each time his hand came up.

She watched the crowd instead of him now. How fast they moved. Whether they shouted the parts back. When the band hit the breaks—a quick stop—the room shouted the line.

Jimmy came in again on the drums.

The song stretched longer than the original version. Joe walked the stage shaking the maracas overhead. The bass player kept stepping toward his microphone for the call and response.

Claire bobbed her head with the beat.

The lights stayed dim. Jimmy was still mostly a silhouette.

The set ended a few songs later.

Joe thanked everyone and said the next band's name.

People clapped and moved toward the floor again.

Claire went to the door.

Outside, the night air was cool. The band was already carrying their equipment to the cars.

The guitar player had a car parked along the curb. The bass player's father stood beside a station wagon with the back open, smoking and watching them load the amplifier.

Joe's girlfriend had borrowed her family's car. She leaned against the door while Joe dropped the maracas into a case.

Everyone was talking at once.

They were laughing.

Claire waited near the sidewalk until Jimmy came out with the snare drum.

He saw her and grinned, still a little breathless.

"You hear that?" Joe said to nobody in particular. "They went crazy."

They packed the last of the gear into the vehicles.

Someone slammed a lid.

Claire slid into the back seat of the guitar player's car and moved over when Jimmy climbed in beside her and put his arm across her shoulders.

It was warm.

The windows were down.

Everyone was still talking about the set.

Claire leaned back against Jimmy's arm and listened.

It was one of the best nights she could remember.

Maggie bought a small row house in Baltimore Highlands, just over the county line, with the insurance money from Eddie's death. The houses were brick and attached, but each one had a narrow strip of yard behind it. Her boys played out there with the other children on the block. Maggie went to work at the bank five days a week. On Saturdays she went out with friends.

Shortly after she bought the house, she met a sailor stationed in Baltimore. From Wisconsin.

One afternoon Maggie brought Eleanor and Claire to the house.

"Mommy, Teen, this is Charlie."

He stood beside Maggie in the living room. Big shoulders, short blond hair. He held Maggie's arm while she talked. When Eleanor spoke to him, he nodded quickly and smiled too long.

Claire watched him look at her once, then look away.

Maggie said Charlie would be getting out of the Navy soon. They were going to get married. Take the boys. Move to Wisconsin.

By Thanksgiving they were already there.

Maggie asked Eleanor to make the trip up for Thanksgiving.

Eleanor and Claire took the bus. Hugh stayed home.

It took twenty-one hours.

They slept sitting up. Each of them had the empty seat beside them for most of the ride. Claire looked at magazines and watched the other passengers.

In Chicago, the bus filled.

A boy sat down next to her. Older. Maybe college. His hair was long and curly and he wore a long, knitted scarf wrapped twice around his neck. He said he had been ice skating. They talked while the bus moved north through flat, gray fields. As the sun was going down, he looked out the window and said, "I think this is the most grotesque time of day."

Claire thought that sounded poetic. She told him about her boy-friend who played drums in a band. The boy listened, leaning back with his hands in his coat pockets.

When the bus pulled into Maggie's town, Claire and Eleanor stood up.

The boy stayed in his seat. He was going farther north.

Thanksgiving at Maggie's house lasted all afternoon. Maggie had started cooking the day before. The kitchen counters were full—bowls, trays, foil. While Eleanor stood in the doorway, Maggie pointed around the room.

"All the woodwork's painted," she said, hands resting on the doorframe.

The trim was white, like in most Baltimore houses. Maggie explained that in the neighbor houses here in Wisconsin, the natural wood grain showed through varnish.

"My neighbors said it was creative and clever," Maggie added, smiling.

Claire blinked slowly and said, "Why would they think it's clever to paint your woodwork?" Maggie narrowed her eyes at Claire.

Charlie carved the turkey. He handled the knife in dramatic sweeping motions but cut carefully.

"My folks had a bar," he said. "Up by the Canadian border. That's where I grew up. Behind the bar."

He laid another slice of turkey onto the platter.

"My dad was German. My mom was Canadian Indian."

Eleanor looked at him for a moment. "You must look like your father," she said.

Charlie laughed. "Yeah, that's what everybody says."

They had two tables set up. The regular dining room table for the adults and a card table with a tablecloth on it for the small children. Maggie told Claire that she had to sit at the children's table "because there's just not room at the big table."

Maggie carried another bowl. "Teen, put potatoes on the kids' plates."

Claire reached for it, bumping her elbow into one of the little boys.

"Teen, don't forget the butter," Maggie added, hands full of bowls, moving around the table.

Claire muttered, "Yes, Mommy." Maggie looked over her shoulder at Claire and made a face.

She sat at the little table, in a little chair, with her knees up too high. She tried to make the boys laugh while passing the plates.

Charlie told another story while carving, and Maggie laughed.

Later, in the small bedroom down the hall, Claire whispered to Eleanor, "What does she see in him?"

Eleanor put a finger to her lips. "Security."

Claire made a face.

"Eww."

86 You Look So Innocent

There was a time when Claire would not have considered cutting school. Jimmy cut whenever he felt like it. It seemed ordinary to him. School was dull. The risk of Eleanor finding out felt smaller than a full day of classes.

Claire left the house at the usual time. She met Jimmy up by the movie theater. They walked two blocks to a small house. Jimmy knocked. Someone opened the door without asking who it was.

Inside, about a dozen kids were scattered through the living room. Records played. People smoked, talked, laughed.

Claire paused just inside the doorway. She did not know anyone. A few of them looked up when Jimmy came in.

"Hi Jimmy."

He kept his arm around her and steered her toward an open space on the floor.

At first, she thought everyone was smoking regular cigarettes. After a minute she noticed the smell. Some of them were joints. They moved slowly from hand to hand. When one reached her, she passed it along without taking any. She hoped no one noticed. People lay back against the wall. A few sat cross-legged on the floor. Two boys stood by the window talking about something that sounded important to them. The room felt hidden and intimate.

After a while Claire stopped watching the door. When the joint came to her again she took a small puff. She coughed immediately. Jimmy laughed.

"Here," he said. "Drink this. It helps."

He handed her a bottle of peppermint schnapps.

She took a swallow, felt it burn and waited for the coughing to stop, and passed the bottle along.

A boy Claire hadn't seen before stood up from the arm of the couch. He was older than the rest of them. Eighteen, maybe more.

"The people who live here are coming back," he said. "We better go." No one argued.

"Let's go out to the quarry."

Claire looked at Jimmy. She had no idea how they would get there.

Outside, parked along the curb, was an old ambulance. The paint
was dull and the red light on top was cracked. It was not the tall kind,
more like an oversized station wagon or a hearse.

"That's mine," the older boy said.

The back doors opened. Kids climbed in. There were no benches.
They all squeezed into the space where a patient would have been on a
stretcher. Claire followed Jimmy inside. Someone handed her the pint
bottle of schnapps.

"Can you put this in your pocketbook?"
She opened her shoulder bag. It was just big enough. The bottle slid inside.
Jimmy watched her close the flap.

"You look so innocent," he said. "Nobody would ever think you had it."

She snapped the clasp shut and set the bag in her lap. The back doors
closed and the ambulance started up.

They drove out into the county. Houses thinned out. The road
turned narrower. After a while the ambulance stopped along a dirt shoulder.
They got out and followed a narrow path through a stand of trees. The
quarry opened suddenly beyond them. The pit was deep and filled with
still water. Pale stone walls rose straight up from the edge. Claire had
heard about kids swimming there but had never seen it. Large rocks sat
along the rim, worn smooth in places from people sitting on them.

The group spread out. Claire and Jimmy found a flat rock a little
away from the others. They sat close together. After a minute he leaned
toward her and they started kissing. The water below was quiet. The quarry
walls rose straight up from the water, pale and cut clean.

A couple of boys climbed down toward the water. One of them
threw a small rock and watched the rings spread across the surface. Someone farther down the rocks checked a watch.

"Hey. We better go. School's letting out soon."

Everyone stood up slowly. The rule was simple: you got home at the
same time you normally would. Then nobody asked questions.

Claire wasn't worried.

Eleanor worked until five.

Hugh wouldn't notice anyway.

87 Sorority

Claire had never heard of sororities in high school until Gina mentioned them. She thought that was something for college. In Baltimore, when adults asked each other where they went to school, they didn't mean college. They meant high school. So, a high school sorority didn't seem as strange as it first sounded.

A friend of Gina's belonged to one. They were holding an afternoon tea where the sorority sisters would look over girls who might pledge.

Claire went with Gina.

The room smelled like perfume and cake. A table was set with three-tiered trays of petit fours and little triangular cucumber sandwiches with the crusts cut off. There were china teacups and saucers, tea poured from matching teapots. The sorority girls moved around the tables studying everyone the way teachers did the first week of school—quietly deciding things.

Both Gina and Claire were invited to pledge.

At the first meeting, the rules were explained. For two weeks the pledges couldn't wear makeup. They couldn't wash their hair. No stockings—only socks. After that there would be "Hell Night," a long night of hazing before induction. Until then the pledges had to do whatever the big sisters told them. Picking things up. Carrying packages. Running small errands. For two weeks, they belonged to the sisters.

Claire went along with it for a week.

She hated not washing her hair. She hated not wearing makeup even more. Without her eyeliner she felt unfinished, like someone had erased the last line of a drawing. Most of the girls in the sorority didn't interest her much either. Except Gina.

S   he told Gina first, then told her assigned big sister she was dropping out. The girl shrugged, a trace of disdain. It didn't matter much. Gina didn't hold it against her.

That was the only part Claire cared about. She washed her hair that night and put her eyeliner back on. Things went back to normal. She still saw Gina when she was over at Jimmy's house.

Sometimes she met school friends at the sub shop around the corner from the dime store. They sat in the booth by the window and watched the cars go by while the jukebox played.

One Saturday afternoon, after leaving her friends, she stopped at the dime store and bought a spool of thread and a bar of Yardley lavender soap.

On the way home she had to pass the corner where the boys stood around on the sidewalk. Gina's boyfriend Tony was there. He was often at Jimmy's house when Claire was there. As Claire came closer she looked down and walked a little more carefully.

"Hey Claire," Tony called. "Open your jacket."

She stopped and looked up. "What?"

"Show us the lining."

She relaxed a little then. Tony had heard her talking about sewing before. She thought he wanted to see the inside of the jacket.

She unbuttoned the jacket and held it open so they could see. She had on a ribbed poor-boy sweater underneath.

The boys started snickering.

Tony turned to them, laughing.

"See," he said. "I told you she had big ones."

Claire buttoned the jacket again and walked on, the boys still laughing behind her.

88 Laundry

A first: a different home, but the same school. The apartment Hugh and Eleanor found was not far from the school. The route changed, but it wasn't any farther to get to class on time. It was a little farther from Jimmy's house.

It was an older apartment complex. Claire didn't remember living in one before, unless you counted the projects. Each square brick building had four two-bedroom apartments. They lived on the first floor. Claire had her own room. Hugh and Eleanor shared the other. The buildings sat in rows with lawns between them. The whole place faced a golf course. Every other building had a laundry room. Their laundry room was in the basement of the building next door.

Before this place, Eleanor had an old round washing machine with a wringer on top. It lived in the kitchen. When it was time to wash clothes, she hooked the hose to the sink. The clothes were hung outside to dry. Here, you fed coins into the washer and dryer.

Most weeks the laundry was Claire's job. She carried the hamper next door and went down to the basement. The room was quiet except for the machines. Light came in through the small windows near the ceiling. Sometimes she brought a magazine and waited for the wash to finish. Sometimes she left and came back when it was time to move the clothes to the dryer.

Next door, her own room waited. Claire was allowed to have Jimmy in her room with the door shut. Sometimes Eleanor would come in without knocking, just to look around. Claire had a television, an extension phone, her sewing machine, and her records. Magazine pictures were pinned to a bulletin board. She made pillow covers in colors she liked, and hung posters on the walls.

She and Jimmy went to the movies or to concerts almost every week. Neither of them had a car, but Jimmy had friends who did and they were usually willing to drive.

They still walked a lot. Sometimes they cut across the golf course back to the old neighborhood.

For band practice, the bass player's father picked them up. He was old and hard of hearing and often fell asleep in a chair while they played. The bass player was younger than Claire and Jimmy and couldn't drive yet. Claire was the only girlfriend who went to practice; Jimmy brought her along. Rehearsals were after hours in an office where the guitar player's mother worked as a secretary.

Claire watched everything.

She started making suggestions about what they should wear on stage. Bands weren't wearing matching suits anymore. Everyone wore something different on stage. She suggested the guitar player and bass player lower their instruments, lengthen the straps, wear them near their hips like the Yardbirds or Hendrix. She said that if they couldn't find the right clothes in stores, she could make them.

Jimmy was the first to let her try.

She made him a shirt for playing. Off-white unbleached muslin. Ruffles down the front and on the bottom of the sleeves. It tied at the neck and had hand embroidery along the opening.

She liked the way it came out.

The rest of the band liked it, too. Soon, she was making clothes for all of them—velvet jackets, altered pants, things they couldn't buy anywhere.

Claire never missed a rehearsal.

She studied musicians at concerts and in magazines. Sometimes she went downtown to buy music and fashion magazines from Europe. She held the bag tight against her side on the way home, the edges of the magazines pressing through the paper. Once, when she stood too long at a newsstand, the grumpy old man behind it said, "Are you reading or buying?"

Claire was buying.

The magazines were expensive. She chose carefully.

89 Crystal Ship

Claire had an endless run of sore throats. Strep. Bronchitis. Tonsillitis. Pneumonia three times before she was fifteen. Antibiotics. Chest X-rays. Waiting rooms with the pungent odor of antiseptics and bleach. The doctor said when this sore throat cleared up, they would schedule a tonsillectomy.

Claire thought tonsils came out when you were little.

Eleanor said sometimes older kids had to have it done too. The older you were, the worse it was.

The doctor said it was time.

Her friends said she would get to eat a lot of ice cream.

When she woke after surgery her throat burned and the back of her throat felt packed with dry gauze. Her head was slow and thick. The nurse told her to be careful. There were stitches in her throat.

Claire asked about ice cream.

The nurse said popsicles or sherbet. No real ice cream because it was made from milk. Milk made mucus.

Claire closed her eyes again. They gave her the pain medicine through the IV because she couldn't swallow pills yet. When she left the hospital, they gave her a small brown bottle of codeine tablets with a white cap.

At home, Eleanor settled Claire in bed. The record player sat on the chair beside her so she could reach it without getting up. Claire swallowed a codeine pill with water and put the Doors album on the turntable.

The needle dropped.

"Break On Through" came in sharp and fast.

Claire slid deeper into the pillow. The mattress held her weight in a slow, heavy way, like it had been waiting for her all day. When she stopped moving, she could feel every place the bed touched her—shoulders, hips, the back of her head.

Her throat hurt less when she didn't swallow.

"Soul Kitchen" followed. The circus-like organ music, sharp and brash, cut against her quiet room. The room seemed quieter than usual, the music sitting in the middle of it. The light at the window looked softer, almost gray.

By the time "The Crystal Ship" began, the codeine had settled in.

Before you slip into unconsciousness
I'd like to have another kiss.

Jim Morrison's voice sounded close to the bed, like he was standing somewhere in the room. Claire turned her head on the pillow and watched the record turning.

The crystal ship is being filled
A thousand girls, a thousand thrills.

The words moved slowly past her, the way clouds moved when she lay on her back, staring up at them.

When the needle reached the end and began tapping softly, the scratching sound woke her enough to reach over and turn the record.

The movement felt important. Needle up. Record over. Needle down.

More songs drifted through the room. "Light My Fire." "The End." Music moving in and out of sleep.

When Morrison said *Father I want to kill you,* Claire turned the volume up.

Sometimes she woke in the middle of a song she already knew.

The days are bright and filled with pain.

Her throat felt dry and tight again. She turned the record and slept. Two days passed that way. Songs, sleep, the slow turn of the record. On the third afternoon Eleanor came in carrying a bowl of chicken noodle soup. She stood in the doorway for a moment listening to the music.

"Codeine isn't good for you," she said. "I'm taking the rest of the bottle."

Claire pushed herself up on one elbow.

"My throat hurts. The doctor said I can't take aspirin."

Eleanor picked up the bottle from the nightstand and slipped it into her pocket.

"I'll bring more soup later."

She left and closed the door behind her.

The record kept playing.

Claire waited for the song to end.

The record turned.

The needle found the groove again.

90 Expulsion

Going back to school after the tonsils came out was worse than before.
She cut gym.

In math she watched the light move across the desks and let the
numbers pass by.

In geography she drew in the margins of her notebook.

It was near the end of the year now. The windows were open. Outside,
the air moved through the trees and carried sounds from the street. It
made the classroom feel smaller. Like the real world was somewhere just
past the brick wall.

Miss Skinner had become a problem. She watched Claire more than
the others.

Claire bent over her notebook, working the pencil back and forth
to darken a shadow along the edge of a face. She was trying to get it right.
The shading had to soften into the paper.

She didn't notice the teacher walking down the aisle.

A hand appeared on the desk.

"Give it to me."

Claire looked up. Miss Skinner stood over her, palm open.

"Give me the piece of paper."

Claire glanced at the drawing. Then back at the teacher.

"No," she said. "It's mine."

Miss Skinner's face reddened. Her hand stayed out, unmoving.

"Give me the piece of paper."

Claire stared at it for a second. Then she tore the page from the notebook.

She tore it again.

And again.

When the drawing was in small pieces she threw them at the teacher.
The pieces fluttered down and settled across the floor between them.

The next thing she knew she was sitting in the principal's office.
Eleanor arrived not long after, as if she had been moving fast through
the building. Claire realized the school must have called her away from
work. A strand of her hair had come loose and was stuck to the side of her
face. She kept pushing it back and then forgetting about it. Her handbag

slipped from her shoulder, and she caught it and set it in her lap.

The unfairness of it settled in Claire all at once. Heat moved up her neck. She clenched her jaw to keep from shouting or running out of the room.

Eleanor looked from Claire to the principal and back again. The principal sat behind his desk with his hands folded on a stack of papers. He spoke without looking at Claire very long. The school did not want Claire there anymore. She was sixteen now. They were not required to keep her.

She was being expelled.

Eleanor tried to reason with him. She leaned forward in the chair, her voice tight. The principal listened without interrupting, then glanced at the clock on the wall and straightened the papers in front of him. Finally, it was clear: Claire would leave that day and not come back.

Eleanor asked if Claire could transfer to another school. "No other school will want her either," the principal said.

They walked out into the hallway.

Eleanor's hands were shaking. She balled up her fists as if that might stop it. Her mouth moved once before any sound came out. Claire walked beside her, silent and hard, anger sitting low in her chest.

When they got home Claire went straight to her room and shut the door.

In the kitchen Eleanor's cards began to shuffle. Claire knew the sound. The soft slide of the deck, then the small click as Eleanor turned them over one at a time on the table. She always laid them out slowly like that.

The apartment stayed quiet until Hugh came home from work.

Claire heard the door open. His boots on the hardwood floor.

Eleanor told him what had happened at the school. Their voices stayed low. From her room Claire could hear the rhythm of the conversation but not every word. After a while Hugh said his niece Ramona made a good living as a beautician. She had her own salon in Pennsylvania. Eleanor said it was a good profession for a girl.

Chairs moved in the kitchen.

A moment later Eleanor knocked on Claire's door. Claire opened it and followed her back to the kitchen.

"You are going to have to work if you can't go to school," Eleanor said. Claire stood beside the table. "We think we could pay for you to go to beauty school."

Claire nodded once.

They said they would find out about it tomorrow.

Claire went back to her room.

Fifteen hundred hours and the state board exam. That was what it took to be a hairdresser. Claire liked the idea of designing haircuts and working somewhere connected to fashion. The course was nine months.

There was a school kit. It came in a small suitcase. Inside were hair shears and thinning shears, a straight razor, manicure tools, a plastic shampoo cape, and other things. There was also a textbook: *Revised Standard Textbook of Cosmetology.* The cover was blue with black lettering and a shadowy drawing of a woman's head with a sideswept flip. Claire liked the book. She liked the kit. She did not like that the students had to wear white uniforms.

Some parts of beauty school were good. She liked learning the proper way to do a manicure. She was good at facial massage and masques. She learned to cut hair quickly—sectioning it into a neat map, clipping each section up, letting down small pieces and snipping them to the right length and shape. They practiced on mannequins: just a head with hair. The students could cut it, perm it, color it, style it.

Claire wanted real people. Stylish young people in a modern salon.

The clients who came in were not that. They were neighborhood ladies with thinning gray hair who brought magazine pictures of complicated hairstyles and expected to leave looking like the picture. Claire was told to work on wigs. She needed more hours before she could work on clients.

Jimmy and his sister Gina were finished with school, too. Jimmy had already quit. One of his Italian grandmother's friends got him a job at a factory that made expensive men's suits. He started as a presser, working a hot steam press all day. That was the lowest job on the sewing room floor. The highest was cutter. Only the most experienced were trusted with the imported fabric. Jimmy thought if he stayed, he would learn new things and move up.

Since last Christmas, it began to seem inevitable that they would get engaged. One night they were watching Rudolph the Red-Nosed Reindeer at Jimmy's. His grandmother was asleep. Everyone else was out. The room was dark except for the blue light from the screen. The stop-motion reindeer moved stiffly across the snow.

Jimmy sat beside her on the couch.

Claire said, "We could go to the basement."

Jimmy looked at her.

"Are you sure?"

"Yes."

They turned the television off.

Just before her curfew Jimmy walked her home. He stayed close, letting her keep the pace, letting her set the rhythm. The streetlights made long shadows across the sidewalk.

Getting home before Eleanor's deadline was still agonizing. Claire realized that Eleanor did, in fact, like Jimmy. But neither she nor Hugh thought he was right for her. They were always pleasant to him. It was hard not to be. Jimmy was easy to like. He was a simple guy, but people liked him. There was something open and positive about him. He made people feel like the world was a good place.

He said things like, "I'd be more than happy to help with that." Claire thought that sounded awful. How could you be more than happy? He told corny jokes. When they got pizza to go he would say, "Cut it into six pieces, I don't think I could eat eight." Then he would laugh. If someone said, "It's nice out." Jimmy would say "Yeah, it's nice out, I think I'll leave it out." Claire would roll her eyes.

Gina had quit school and gotten a job downtown. She didn't work at the brokerage where her mother and sisters were secretaries. You had to finish high school for that. Her job was a block away in a small office on the second floor of an old building. Two middle-aged men and one gal Friday. Gina typed well. She knew how to deal with people. She did fine there. She was still going with Tony. She said they were going to get married.

Now that Claire was going to be a hairdresser—with a real career—she decided to pierce her ears whether Eleanor approved or not. She knew better than to let a friend do it with a needle. If it got infected Eleanor would never stop talking about it. She found a doctor who would pierce them for a reasonable price. Jimmy bought her a pair of tiny solid gold hoop earrings.

Once it was done there was not much Eleanor could say.

It went onto Eleanor's list of disappointments.

Claire had combed and styled the same wig six times. She had proven she could do finger waves. Nobody wore finger waves anymore. They belonged to the 1920s. She had done manicures on dozens of customers. They all chose the same shade of pink. She had learned to do permanents with the little plastic curlers and papers on the ends. The solution smelled terrible. People were ironing their hair straight now, not getting permanents. The whole thing seemed ridiculous.

Gina had married Tony at the courthouse. Just the two of them. She told Claire she was pregnant and didn't want anyone to know yet. She was going to quit her job. If Claire wanted it, Gina was sure she could get it.

Claire thought about not wearing a white uniform. She thought about earning money instead of Eleanor and Hugh paying her tuition. She thought about putting neighborhood women's hair into French twists with barrel curls on top and more manicures with the same shade of pink. She wanted to create beauty, not follow instructions. She was done.

She told the head of the school she was quitting.

"But you nearly have enough hours to work with the customers," the woman said.

Claire didn't change her mind.

Claire went home and changed her clothes, leaving before Eleanor got home from work. Jimmy was still at work, too.

She got on a bus and went downtown. She got off at Mount Vernon Square. People were gathered in the park. Boys and girls with long hair. Colorful clothes. Beads. Some barefoot.

Claire walked past them slowly. A few said, "Peace," and smiled. She smiled back and kept walking. It was hard to believe this was the same park she had played in after piano lessons at Peabody when she was little.

Claire walked to Read Street where the boutiques were. She looked in the windows and went into a few stores. The Bead Experience had bell bottom jeans, suede jackets with long fringe and beads hanging everywhere. She wanted half the store. She imagined getting a paycheck and coming back.

A little farther down the block she saw a bookstore. She went in.

Near the register, in a glass case, a yellow box caught her eye. Black letters on the box said Tarot Cards. She stood looking at them for a moment. Then she knew she had to have them.

She dug all the change out of the bottom of her purse and added her lunch money for the week. It was just enough. "Good choice," the clerk said, putting the cards into a small paper bag. Claire put the bag in her purse and went to the bus stop.

At home she took the cards to her room. She looked at them over and over. The blue and white plaid backs. The colorful pictures on the fronts. There were more cards than in a regular deck. She laid some of them out the way Eleanor did when she read cards. Eleanor would not approve. [Why not?] Claire hid them where Eleanor would not see them. When she heard Eleanor's key in the door she realized she still had to tell her about beauty school.

She told Eleanor that evening.

Eleanor looked at her for a long moment.

"You quit."

"Yes."

"You don't care if I work myself to death!"

Eleanor slapped her. She had done it before. Claire slapped her back this time.

"I hate you!"

Eleanor stood holding her cheek. Neither of them spoke.

Claire went to her room. The door shut.

Claire got the job. She was the new gal Friday at Badenhorst & Westheimer, a foreign freight forwarding company. The company handled paperwork between companies in different countries. From the messages clattering out of the teletype machine, Claire gathered that they shipped a lot of tractors to Vietnam.

She was not as good a typist as Gina. Sometimes the teletypes came out garbled.

Two middle-aged men worked in the office with her. The nicer one was Mr. Horst. He was quiet, soft-looking. A photograph of his wife and daughter stood on his desk. The other one was Mr. McClanahan.

Mr. McClanahan was huge—tall and heavy. He smoked thick cigars and drank at lunch. When he spoke to Claire he often used double entendres. She pretended not to notice. When he came back from lunch, he sometimes grabbed her. She slid away from the desk and he followed her around it.

Once she told Eleanor.

"Oh, most bosses do that," Eleanor said. "Mr. Eli at the sweatshop used to pat all of us girls on the butt."

Claire was horrified.

Mr. McClanahan asked several times why Gina had quit. Gina had told him she was getting married and wanted to be a housewife. She did not want him to know she was pregnant. Claire repeated the same story.

"She's not pregnant yet?" He asked once.

Claire shook her head.

Every Friday they handed Claire her check before lunch so she could cash it.

Most days she ate lunch at the Read's counter near the office. Small jukeboxes lined the counter. Wherever you sat you could play a song. She chose songs about other places. "If You're Going to San Francisco." "California Dreamin'." She never spoke to anyone. On Fridays she cashed her check, kept enough for bus fare and lunches, and spent most of the rest on clothes. There was a boutique close enough to reach during lunch.

She still lived in the apartment with Eleanor and Hugh but was often at Jimmy's.

Jimmy's family gathered regularly at his parents' house for dinner. Claire was usually there, too.

After Jimmy's little Irish grandmother died, Vince and Kathleen moved to a new townhouse farther out toward the county. Only two of their children still lived at home. They were close enough to Mama Dear for her to bring food over a few times a week.

Claire had finally met everyone. Before the first visit Jimmy told her, "Just don't mention you're not Catholic." Vince and his mother spoke Italian together. Claire did not understand any of it. The only English word she heard Mama Dear say was "Sonofabitch," all one word.

Gina and Tony were married now and had their own apartment. Gina's pregnancy was beginning to show. Sandy was engaged to Scotty Kapuscinski. Josie had already been married and living in her own house with a husband and little boy before Claire met Jimmy. Robert was out of the Army and had a place of his own.

Dinner at the Marinos was loud. At Claire's house her parents had read books at the table while she read hers. The room had been quiet. The Marinos talked over each other. Vince shouted even when he was not angry. If someone asked, "Where's the salt?" he pointed to his nose and yelled, "It's uppa here! Wanna come get it!?"

The others laughed.

Claire felt her stomach knot.

Under the table the toy poodle, Fifi, waited for something to fall.

PART FIVE

Jimmy gave Claire an engagement ring for Christmas. It was the one she had pointed out in the jewelry store window. There was no proposal scene. By then it was understood. They already moved through the world as a pair—part of each other's families, making small decisions about the future as if the larger ones were already settled.

Bride's magazines began appearing on the coffee table. Claire and Eleanor looked through them together and talked about dresses, flowers, the reception hall. It would be a traditional wedding. Claire was sixteen, so her parents would have to sign the papers. The date would be sometime the following year.

One thing was clear from the beginning. The wedding would be at St. Boniface, for Jimmy's family. The question of Claire converting to Catholicism came up almost immediately.

Claire had no interest in joining the Catholic Church, or any church. Still, St. Boniface was a beautiful building, and she knew it mattered to Jimmy's parents. She made an appointment with the priest to ask about having the ceremony there.

Teenage weddings were common in their part of Baltimore. Many couples married right after high school. It was a blue-collar city, a time when girls were raised to become wives. If you had a decent trade waiting, most people saw no reason to go to college. Sons went to the same plants or shops where their fathers worked. Daughters married boys from the neighborhood and set up house nearby. The pattern repeated itself quickly.

Gina, who was Claire's age, was already married. Jimmy's friends Paula and Rick had married the year before, and they were only a year older than Claire. Elsewhere people might wait until their twenties, but here it was not unusual for a sixteen-year-old girl to be planning a wedding.

Claire's days settled into a routine. She went to the office job where the dirty old man chased her around the desks, planned the wedding with Eleanor, went to movies or concerts with Jimmy, and sometimes sat through band practice in his parents' basement. At home she sewed or read.

When she went to the newsstands downtown to look for magazines she lingered longer than she needed to, knowing she might get the side-eye from the owner for dawdling. At first, she bought the usual ones, but gradually she began picking up magazines from other countries. She liked looking at the clothes and the faces—people who did not look like anyone she knew. She also liked watching the people on the bus and on the sidewalks between her neighborhood and downtown, where things felt less fixed.

Eleanor listened politely when Claire talked about those things, but they were not subjects she had much to add to. She preferred talking about family history and the practical details of adult life—good china, a proper silver service, what Claire should register for before the wedding.

Claire nodded through these conversations. What she imagined for herself was different. She wanted to travel. She had the steady feeling that something important was happening somewhere else.

Jimmy's band had been changing, too. A new guitar player had joined, and they were still trying to settle on a bass player. That position turned over regularly. About once a month someone new would haul an amplifier down the steps into Jimmy's parents' basement and try out while the rest of them played.

Recently they had added a keyboard player with a small Farfisa organ that made a thin, squeaky sound. During breaks, Claire sometimes walked past and pressed a few keys. She liked the bright, bouncing chords at the beginning of "96 Tears" and would play them quickly before moving on.

No one, not even Claire, thought she might actually play in the band. The only girls she knew of in bands were singers. Claire didn't sing. She liked being there—watching them rehearse, making clothes for them to wear on stage.

Military tanks were moving down the main road beyond the field. A long line of them. No other traffic. Claire stood on the apartment steps holding a laundry basket on her way to the laundry room next door. She had stopped halfway down the steps to watch them pass. She counted them as they went by.

In Baltimore the tension between Black and White neighborhoods had always been there. When Martin Luther King was assassinated on April 4, it broke open. Riots spread through cities across the country, and Baltimore's were some of the worst.

Troops came into the city by the thousands. A curfew was declared. Martial law.

On television, there were pictures of smashed store windows and people carrying armfuls of merchandise into the street. Grocery stores, appliance shops, furniture stores, liquor stores, pawn shops. Fires burned along whole blocks. Cars were overturned. Snipers fired at police, firemen, and National Guard soldiers.

People stayed home from work and school. Hugh and Eleanor talked about the senseless destruction and the small businesses that would never reopen. Soldiers stood at intersections with rifles. At dusk, the firehouse sirens sounded for the curfew.

Claire had friends who had been drafted and sent to Vietnam. Now tanks were rolling past the field near her home.

The riots went on for three days.

When it was over, six people were dead. Hundreds were injured. Thousands were arrested. More than a thousand businesses were damaged or destroyed. Whole blocks were burned out. Many stores never opened again.

Afterward, many White families moved to the county. Eleanor did the opposite. She found an apartment closer in town.

They moved to Waverly, a working-class neighborhood not far from Charles Village, where Bucky lived. Eleanor also found a small apartment nearby for her mother, Annie Mae. Annie Mae was on welfare and it wasn't easy to find something affordable, but Eleanor managed it.

After getting her high school equivalency certificate, Eleanor had gradually moved into better jobs. Now she worked as a long-distance operator for the Chesapeake and Potomac Telephone Company. The building was in Charles Village, near Annie Mae's place, not far from Bucky, and within walking distance from the new apartment.

Hugh never seemed to care where they lived. If it were up to him, they would have a camper and travel around in it.

The wedding plans were moving faster.

Claire had begun to feel that the wedding wasn't hers anymore. Mama Dear had decided the reception would be in the church hall at her parish in Little Italy. In the Marino family, Mama Dear's decisions were final.

Eleanor told Claire to go along with it. If the reception was there, the Marinos would pay for it. Eleanor, Hugh, and Claire would cover the rest—the ceremony, the clothes, the flowers, and the church fee.

Claire mentioned that she wanted a long mantilla veil. Eleanor said that would look terrible on her. Instead, she should wear a long white dress with a full veil and short gloves. The wedding would be in summer, two months after her seventeenth birthday.

Claire sat in front of the desk. The priest's eyes scanned her like she was damaged merchandise.

Jimmy sat beside her. He had grown up in this church. His first communion had been here. For a short time, he had even been an altar boy. His whole family was Catholic. In his mind he had always expected to be married at St. Boniface.

The first question was conversion.

It would be easier, the priest said, if Claire converted to Catholicism.

Claire said she would not.

She believed in God. She believed she could speak to God herself. She had no intention of accepting the idea that she needed a man in a backward collar to do the talking for her.

When it became clear she would not convert, the priest explained the next step. Because Claire was not Catholic, they would need a special dispensation from the bishop to marry.

After that, they would attend marriage preparation classes.

Claire did not mind those classes.

If the bishop approved, they could marry in the church. They would have to sign a promise to raise all children Catholic. They would have to skip the full nuptial mass. Her ceremony would be shorter. No birth control if either partner was Catholic. Pills were nearly impossible for unmarried girls under twenty-one. Claire knew Catholic girls who took them. Hypocrites.

Claire signed the papers. The whole arrangement felt like a scam. More Catholic babies. More money. It didn't seem to have much to do with God. Signing it felt like writing her own excuse note for gym class—and signing her mother's name.

In the classes Claire asked a lot of questions. Not because she was confused, but because she wanted them to admit they were wrong. They never did.

Jimmy was mildly annoyed by the process, but more than Claire, he was used to doing what he was told.

There were choices to be made. A wedding to produce.

Uncle Leroy had died that spring, back in western Pennsylvania. Hugh went up for a few days. When he came back, he was quieter as if a piece of him was missing. There was no one else like Leroy to call.

Claire, Eleanor, and Jimmy's sisters went dress shopping on Eastern Avenue. The hub for bridal shopping. A Baltimore tradition.

They walked past rows of shop windows. Mannequins in stiff lace stared back. The smell of flowers and perfume filled the air. Salesgirls hovered at counters, measuring, pinning, adjusting. Small groups jostled past with chatter about fittings and alterations. The avenue had a rhythm: satin rustling, lace whispering, orders being written on yellow slips. It was all very precise, very traditional, very Baltimore.

Dresses were chosen from samples, then ordered. The racks held one size, small to medium. Larger girls squeezed in; the dresses didn't zip. They guessed how it would look. Very petite girls stood in fabric that hung like bags; pins and clips pulled it back so they could see the shape. Almost every bride left feeling wrong in her body.

Claire was a curvy medium. Dresses were tight in the hips or baggy at the waist. Popular styles used abundant lace, chiffon, or satin. Claire did not like shiny. This was a summer wedding. She wanted linen or cotton pique. White, unquestioned, even though it washed her out.

She let the others pick the main colors. They had to wear the dresses. She had long since lost control to Eleanor anyway. The bridesmaids chose yellow empire-waist A-line dresses with a double pleat in the back. The maid of honor wore the same dress in mint green.

Claire's dress was floor length, linen, with Venetian lace trim. A simple empire-waist A-line like the bridesmaids', only with a single long pleat in front and a short train that buttoned to the seam in back. She would have chosen differently for another wedding, but for a traditional one, she liked it.

She lifted the hem and let it brush the floor. White made her pale. She would fix that with a touch of makeup.

She stood back and studied herself in the mirror. Linen, lace, the soft pleat in front. Traditional. Predictable. But hers. She would wear it, and she would make it hers.

Bucky took medication every day to keep the voices away. He had a small basement apartment near Johns Hopkins University. Claire and Jimmy went to visit him there.

The apartment had a kitchen, a bathroom, and one large room. The walls were lined with bookshelves. The room looked like a small library.

Jimmy asked if Bucky had read all the books.

"Yes. Every one of them."

When Claire stepped closer, she saw that each shelf held two rows. The shelves were deeper than they first appeared. A second row of books stood neatly behind the first.

She slid one book out. *One Flew Over the Cuckoo's Nest* by Ken Kesey.

Bucky received a military pension. He had been medically discharged from the Marines and before that had served a full term in the Army Special Forces.

In the hallway between the main room, the bathroom and the kitchen was a print of a painting by Amedeo Modigliani. The woman's face was long and pale, the neck stretched upward, the eyes dark and calm.

Claire asked about it.

Bucky said he had been seeing a graduate student from Johns Hopkins and that her name was Maria.

He did not say much else about her or the painting. Claire looked again at the painting as they passed through the hallway.

A desk stood against the wall with a typewriter on it. Bucky said he had been writing a lot.

He had spent time in Europe and Asia when he was in the Special Forces and some of his tastes reflected that. There was a small statue of Buddha on the desk. He had always been different from the rest of Claire's family and from the people Claire and Jimmy knew.

He spoke to Claire the same way he spoke to adults. He always had, even when she was a child.

Jimmy's brother Robert had come out of the military with problems, too. Claire was never clear how his condition was described. Robert was quiet, like Bucky.

On television, Claire had seen people protesting the draft. After seeing Bucky again, she felt certain that she agreed with them. She wanted to join the protests she had heard about.

Claire and Jimmy walked around Bucky's neighborhood before they left. It felt different from theirs. People moved differently there, easier in their bodies, relaxed but purposeful.

Along the commercial strip there was a bookstore. In the window were books Claire wanted to read.

Jimmy did not read for pleasure. Claire did.

When she got home, she told Eleanor about Bucky's apartment and all the books.

Eleanor was quiet for a moment.

"You know they tested his IQ in the hospital," she said.

Claire asked what the number was.

"One seventy-five."

"That sounds high."

"The average is one hundred," Eleanor said.

So Bucky had been categorized. The military hospital had diagnosed him as a paranoid schizophrenic with a genius IQ. That was how Eleanor explained him to other people.

Claire asked Eleanor what she thought about the anti-military protests.

Eleanor had always spoken about World War II in nostalgic terms. Soldiers were heroes.

"This war might be different," she said.

She did not explain further.

The hairdresser insisted on an updo. Claire thought it was stiff, old-fash-ioned. She looked in the mirror. A large bow sat on top of her head, up-right. It reminded her of the one they made her wear in nursery school that Christmas. She looked like a bride, just not the kind she had imagined.

"My hair looks like a hurricane wouldn't knock it down," she said to Eleanor. "And this bow just adds insult to injury."

Eleanor kept talking. Claire didn't listen.

Everyone else was already at the church. Claire had never been late for anything before. Eleanor was frantic. She had managed to keep Hugh relatively sober since he was supposed to escort Claire down the aisle.

Hugh shrugged. "I just have to get her up there."

They finally left the house, twenty minutes late. Eleanor and Hugh went ahead in their car. Claire followed in the rented limousine.

The church sat on the west side of the street. It was ten in the morning and the sun was already high. The light stone of the building reflected it. Hugh's white jacket reflected it. Claire's dress reflected it. Everything was so bright she had to squint.

She did not feel very bridelike. She felt as if she were in a play. A photographer was waiting outside. He was a friend of the Marino family. He instructed Hugh to help the bride out of the car so he could take a picture.

Hugh had never helped Claire out of anything before that she could remember.

They managed the moment carefully. Hugh took her hand. Claire stepped out of the limousine.

The photographer got his picture. Hugh in his rented tuxedo, look-ing toward the camera, taking Claire's hand as she stepped down. They looked as though they were shaking hands. Claire's smile was arranged. The veil partly hid her expression. The bow stood stiff on the crown of her head.

Eleanor slipped quietly into the church and took her seat in the front pew. Hugh stayed with Claire and the wedding party in the vestibule. Claire looked around. There was a small marble niche filled with holy water. Nearby was a wooden box labeled "Poor Box" where people could leave money for charity. To Jimmy's family, these objects were comforting in their familiarity.

Hugh followed her glance toward the holy water.

"Careful," he muttered quietly. "That's Papist water. Might burn you."

Claire looked at him. They both smirked but did not laugh.

The organ was already playing.

The ushers and bridesmaids went first and arranged themselves across the altar. Then the ring bearer and flower girl followed. People in the pews smiled and leaned toward one another. Soft sounds of approval passed through the church.

When the music changed, Claire and Hugh stepped forward. They walked slowly down the aisle together.

At the altar steps the priest asked the question he had practiced at the rehearsal.

"Who gives this woman to be married to this man?"

"I do," Hugh said, exactly as instructed. He placed Claire's hand in Jimmy's hand and then went to sit beside Eleanor.

Claire felt a small sense of relief standing next to Jimmy. He was still her boyfriend.

The priest began speaking. Claire listened, but the words drifted around her. The ceremony felt slightly dreamlike, as though she were watching it from a distance.

She made all the correct movements. She stood when she was supposed to stand. She knelt when she was supposed to kneel. She repeated the words when it was her turn.

Then the priest asked if anyone objected.

For a moment Claire's mind was completely clear. I do, she thought. I object. None of this is how I wanted it.

But she said nothing.

The ceremony continued.

At the end the organ burst into cheerful music. Claire and Jimmy turned and walked back down the aisle together.

Outside, people threw rice as they passed. They moved quickly through the crowd and into the waiting limousine.

The door shut behind them and the car pulled away.

99   Reception

The reception was in the church hall in Little Italy. The walls were painted warm ochre. Long tables were covered with white cloths and small floral arrangements. At the ends of the tables hung bottles of Chianti in straw. At one end of the room stood the punch fountain. It was silver and tall, with pink liquid bubbling down the sides. Eleanor had insisted on it. She was a teetotaler. She wanted a festive drink for the non-drinkers.

People lined up politely with small paper cups. The punch tasted sweet and harmless. No one hesitated. They drank. The children drank first. Then the adults who had passed on wine.

For a while everything seemed normal. Then the first person slipped quietly toward the bathrooms. Then another. Then another.

No one connected the events at first.

Claire had drunk a cup herself. She felt a little queasy but assumed it was nerves. Weddings were supposed to do that.

Someone finally said it might be the punch.

By then the hallway outside the restrooms was full. People leaned against chairs or held their stomachs. The children were the worst off. One small boy sat on the floor looking pale and confused while his mother fanned him with a napkin.

The punch fountain continued to flow cheerfully.

The people who had drunk wine were fine. They sat calmly at the tables sipping Chianti from small glasses, watching the situation develop with polite interest.

Hugh and Eleanor had not arrived yet. They had been on their way to the reception when a city bus bumped their car in traffic. No one was hurt, but the delay was long enough that the reception had begun without them.

When they finally walked in, the hall was full of pink-faced guests and wobbly children.

It was time to introduce the bride and groom to the crowd. Someone picked up the microphone.

"For the first time ever," the voice announced, "Mr. and Mrs. James Marino!"

Applause filled the room.

The band moved easily from big band swing to Sinatra and Dean Martin. When they played "Mary in the Morning", Kathleen Marino dabbed at her eye and lifted her glass of Chianti.

Claire looked across the room.

There was also a table for the gifts. A few were already there, mostly from Claire's side of the guest list. Eleanor had insisted they register, like proper people do. They had registered, but hardly anyone bought the things on the list.

There was a fondue set. A cookie jar shaped like a rooster. A silver tray. Classic for the times.

Jimmy's family had a different tradition. They gave money. Guests danced with the bride and handed her an envelope during the dance.

Claire did not want to dance with people. She also thought money was a crass gift.

Some of the envelopes ended up on the gift table. Some were handed quietly to Jimmy.

Eleanor straightened the tissue paper around the boxed gifts and lined the envelopes into a neat stack. She looked pleased with the table, as if it had turned out well.

Hugh stood nearby with his hands in his pockets, watching the room.

Claire barely looked at the table again.

Watching her parents, Claire noticed something she had never quite thought about before.

Her own family was stiff. They almost never touched one another. Physical affection was rare enough to feel strange when it happened. Hugh had never once said "I love you" to her in her entire life. The same was true of her siblings.

When she first met the Marinos she had assumed their constant hugging and touching was simply an Italian thing. Partly it was. But partly it was that her own family stood at the opposite extreme.

The culture clash was obvious.

Meanwhile the band played on.

Claire danced when she had to, mostly for photographs and tradition.

People made toasts and clinked their glasses with their cutlery.

She went through the motions.

None of it was her style, or her family's taste.

Cake was cut. The bouquet was thrown. More photographs were taken.

The details blurred together.

By the time they left for the honeymoon, Claire had already forgotten most of it.

The door closed behind them and the reception disappeared as if it had been a rehearsal for something else.

100 Atlantic City

People said Atlantic City was a good place for a honeymoon. This was before the casino era. People came for the beach, the boardwalk, and the big hotels. The weekend was cold. Record-setting cool. Rain all day.

Claire and Jimmy sat in their hotel room and looked at each other.

The hotel brochure described it as a premier Boardwalk hotel, renowned for its French Regency style and sun decks. Jimmy's sister Sandy had recommended it as the perfect honeymoon hotel.

Claire had never stayed in a place like this. When her family traveled, they slept in the car or stayed with relatives. At the beach in Ocean City, she had stayed in a small motel with metal railings and sand in the hallway.

The room had heavy furniture, thick carpet, and curtains that blocked most of the gray daylight. She did not see what the fuss was about. Nothing about it suggested romance. The basement at Jimmy's house, with the drum set and the Christmas lights, had been more convincing.

Jimmy noticed something beside the bed. A metal box with a coin slot. MAGIC FINGERS

Claire studied it cautiously. Jimmy said he thought the bed probably massaged you if you put money in.

Claire put in a quarter. The entire bed began vibrating.

She squealed "Eww!" and jumped off.

Jimmy stood there laughing while the bed rattled violently for several minutes and then stopped on its own.

Jimmy looked at her. "How was it?" he said, trying not to laugh.

Claire said, deadpan, "The earth moved." She pressed her lips together so she wouldn't laugh.

Jimmy lasted about two seconds. Then they both started laughing.

They walked around the hotel to see what people did there. Mostly they drank in the bars or ate in the restaurants.

Jimmy and Claire were too young for the bars. The restaurants required jackets and ties. Jimmy did not own a jacket and tie and had never considered bringing one to the beach. The only place they were welcome was the breakfast restaurant.

At the reception, when Claire told Maggie where they were going for their weekend honeymoon, Maggie leaned close and whispered that Atlantic City was the only beach she knew where interracial couples and queer couples walked around together in public.

Claire assumed that meant it might be interesting. She was wrong. The beach was empty.

Gray water. Low clouds. Rain and wind.

Claire had not brought a sweater. Certainly not an umbrella. They walked the boardwalk looking for a sweater. What they mostly saw were older women in fur coats carrying small dogs.

Several of them. At the beach. In July.

The dogs seemed comfortable with it.

They found a clothing shop that was open. Everything was expensive and serious looking.

Claire bought a sweater from the sale rack that looked like something an old person might wear. It itched.

Jimmy smoked cigarettes while they walked in the drizzle. Then he remembered the Steel Pier.

It was two blocks away. Claire put on the sweater and they went.

The pier had rides, carnival games, and large painted signs advertising the Diving Horse. The horse and its rider climbed a tower and dove into a twelve-foot pool four times a day.

The horse, apparently, declined to perform in the rain. The show was canceled. Most of the pier was closed.

One game booth was open. A baseball game where you knocked down stacked targets to win stuffed animals. The prizes ranged from tiny to enormous.

Jimmy tried.

He knocked down the lowest row and won a small toy. He handed it to Claire.

Then he tried again. Another small toy.

He kept playing. Each time he won one he handed it to Claire. Soon she was holding so many that the situation became impractical.

Teddy bears. Rabbits. Dogs. Eight toys.

Claire suggested that perhaps they had enough animals. Jimmy said he still wanted the large lion on the top shelf.

The pier was nearly empty. Rain and cold wind kept people away.

The man running the booth watched them with growing interest. At first he gave his usual speech and handed over prizes without looking up.

After Jimmy had won every available color of bear, rabbit, and dog, the man leaned on the counter and studied him carefully.

Jimmy paid again.

He held the ball, squinted, and threw as hard as he could. The targets fell.

Only the lowest row. Another small toy.

Claire watched the large lion remain on the shelf.

The man reached up, took down the lion, and handed it to Jimmy.

"Since you're on your honeymoon," he said. "Congratulations."

Thanks!! They both said.

They walked back to the hotel through the steady rain carrying their stuffed animals.

In the room Claire began packing. The animals were lined up across the bed. Bears. Rabbits. Dogs. The lion in the middle.

Jimmy looked at them.

"Better to quit while we're ahead," he said.

They left Atlantic City the next morning with their menagerie.

Claire had never lived in a new building before. Every place she remembered had already been worn down by someone else.

They chose a garden apartment about a mile from Jimmy's grandmother, Mama Dear. Three brick buildings stood around a wide lawn with curved sidewalks. Everything looked recently finished.

They took a two-bedroom so the extra room could be a den. The living room opened into the dining area. The kitchen was smaller than Claire expected and fitted with very modern appliances. It was the first time she had used an electric stove. The floor was sunny yellow and speckled cream vinyl tile, shiny as if it had just been waxed. Claire liked the way it looked.

The rest of the floors were parquet. When Claire brought Eleanor to see the place before the wedding, Eleanor looked down and said, "Oh. Parquet floors," and nodded.

They were starting with almost nothing. At a furniture store downtown, they chose a Spanish revival living room set: an olive green velvet sofa, a gold chair, dark heavy wood tables. Claire thought the Mediterranean look might appeal to Jimmy's family, though they probably didn't care. Jimmy had a steady job, so the store sold it to them on credit.

Eleanor offered to buy their bedroom furniture as a wedding gift. It was another dark set with carved details. Eleanor also bought it on credit.

Claire had been collecting dishes since the engagement and nearly had a full set in a teal-and-gray pattern. She and Jimmy went to Pier 1 Imports for tableware and a bedspread.

Their record collection was the only thing that looked abundant. They put theirs together and it filled a whole wall. Jimmy gave the duplicates to his cousin.

Their tastes overlapped, but were not identical. Claire played Cream, Donovan, and Jefferson Airplane most often. Jimmy preferred Hendrix and Motown. He liked James Brown best.

When they came back from their shortened honeymoon, the apartment felt unusually quiet.

Jimmy kept his drums at his parents' house and practiced there.

Claire had not brought her sewing machine yet. They didn't own a television, so they went out most nights. They still went to the movies every week. They still went to hear bands. Jimmy still had rehearsals.

Claire had quit her job. She expected she would be a good housewife. She was a pretty good cook and she liked arranging things.

During the day the apartment was silent. Jimmy left early for work. Claire played records and read for hours, then by the time Jimmy came home she was restless and ready to go out. He was tired.

She rearranged the apartment again and again. Posters moved from one wall to another; the sofa shifted across the room and back. New towels appeared in the bathroom. The dishes collected in the sink.

At Hugh and Eleanor's house she had only dusted and done the laundry. Eleanor had tried to make her wash dishes, but Claire refused. Eleanor usually did them herself. One afternoon she walked into the kitchen in bare feet and the floor stuck slightly when she stepped. She took another step. It pulled again.

She stood still and looked down at the yellow and cream tiles, not shiny anymore and streaked with unidentifiable substances. She opened the cabinet under the sink. There were no cleaning supplies there. No bucket. No mop. Not even a sponge. She closed the door.

The apartment was completely quiet.

She went into the dining room and sat down on the floor. There was no table yet. They ate at the coffee table in the living room.

After a while she bent forward and cried until she felt sick.

Claire felt like she was losing her mind. The kitchen floor stuck to her feet when she walked across it and she didn't know how to clean it. She called Eleanor about it.

"You made your bed," Eleanor said. "Now lie in it." But on Saturday she came over anyway and helped Claire clean the kitchen.

Jimmy's band was still playing local shows. They won third place in a battle of the bands. Someone gave them a small trophy. The things that had been exciting before seemed smaller now. Claire was happy for him.

There were people in the apartment all the time. A few of Jimmy's friends from way back would show up with beer, sit around and talk about themselves. Their stories ended with "I was so fucked up" or "I guess I told him." They were too young to buy alcohol legally. They found an older guy out in front of the liquor store to get it for them.

Sometimes they brought girlfriends. None of them were really Claire's friends. She noticed the guys didn't hear them or laughed over them. Small, repeated dismissals. She remembered herself, all her life, taken seriously for being smart. And yet these girls weren't ignored because they were stupid. Something else was going on. She watched the others in the room, how the jokes landed, whose voices carried, whose didn't.

Everyone was still under twenty-one. They liked that Jimmy and Claire had a place where they could drink. They liked passing a joint without worrying about parents walking in.

Claire worried about the neighbors. Marijuana was illegal with stiff penalties. People went to jail for having a dime bag in their pocket.

During the day the apartment was quiet. Jimmy was at work.

Claire read books and studied her tarot cards. She found a paperback on astrology at the bookstore near Bucky's apartment. There was much more to it than just "what sign are you" and the newspaper horoscopes. She kept it to herself.

She read *Siddhartha* by Hermann Hesse and *The Prophet* by Kahlil Gibran. There was no one to talk to about those books. She thought Bucky might understand, but he was always in his own world and somehow ahead of her.

Claire's school friends were getting ready for their senior year. She sensed something slipping past her, but not in their plans. Her school friends chattered about graduation and the senior prom. Claire had already left.

During the day the apartment was quiet. Jimmy was at work.

Sometimes Claire took the bus downtown to the main branch of the Enoch Pratt Free Library. The new apartment was farther from the bus line than where she had lived before. She had ridden buses alone all her life, but now she sometimes felt conspicuous, school-age and out during the day.

The neighborhood branch didn't have much. The main branch had better books. There were just enough coins in the couch cushions for bus fare or a soda. She chose bus fare.

It was quiet. Claire didn't pay much attention to the other patrons. She liked asking the librarians questions. They seemed pleased that she was interested and they had answers. She liked that the library didn't cost anything.

Jimmy worked all day and brought home his paycheck on Friday. At first Claire assumed that once you were married, money would somehow take care of itself. After a few weeks she realized it didn't. The refrigerator was empty again by Thursday. The furniture was on credit. She found out that her ring was too. She had assumed Jimmy was taking care of the payments.

He wasn't.

Jimmy left for work. Bag lunch. Jacket. Kiss at the door.

Everything looked normal. But Claire sensed something was wrong. The hallway mailbox held two white business envelopes and one with a red stripe. Gas and electric shut-off notice. She had seen those before, in her parents' house. She hadn't expected one here.

She waited.

Jimmy came home early. He looked rested. No paycheck.

"What do you mean you don't have a paycheck?"

Jimmy's face went red.

"Some of us got laid off last week."

Claire's jaw tightened.

"Then where the hell have you been going every morning?"

"Hanging out with the guys," he said.

"Where?"

"Up by the old place."

"What do you do all day?"

"Play pinball."

"All damn day?"

"Uh… yeah."

She picked up the bills. Slapped them down one by one.

"How could you do this? You've been lying to me."

Jimmy made the face he used when something broke.

"I'm sorry."

"You're sorry?" Her voice went sharp. "What the hell does that mean?"

A knock at the door.

Sal, two other guys, a six-pack. They moved straight into the living room.

Claire followed. She sat in her chair. Breathing heavy. No one noticed.

The stories started. Pool halls. Arguments. Cars. Cousins. Same stories.

Claire laughed louder than usual.

Sal said, "I guess I told him!"

Claire slapped the arm of the chair.

"Hell yeah you did."

Sal blinked. Jimmy glanced at her.

Beer cans snapped open. Pinball talk.

Claire stood.

"How about I get you guys something to eat?"

They brightened. "Yeah!"

She opened the fridge. Empty. A jar of mustard. A gray blob in a jar. She slammed it shut. ....

Oh, I'm sorry," she called. "Looks like we're out of everything."

Jimmy knew the line was for him.

She walked back in.

"Would anybody like to buy a damn pizza?"

Jimmy's eyes darted between Claire and his friends.

Sal shrugged.

"Yeah, we can get a pizza."

Coins and bills clattered on the coffee table. Two crumpled singles. A handful of change.

"You can call it in," Claire said. Kitchen phone. That was usually her job.

Jimmy's mouth tightened. His hands fidgeted.

"Hey, Sal," he said. "Can we borrow your car for a minute?"

Sal tossed him the keys.

"Anything for you, Jimmy."

Jimmy caught them. He signaled Claire. She followed. The door clicked shut behind them.

Claire's hands stayed in her pockets. She let the silence grow. The street was empty. Jimmy fiddled with the keys. He didn't know what she would do next.

She smiled. Just a little.

104 Coda

Jimmy unlocked the passenger side first, let Claire get in and closed the door. He went around the car and sat in the driver's seat.

He said, "You shouldn't cuss in front of people."

She closed her eyes for a second, took a deep breath, both hands to her forehead, then the ceiling of the car, and screamed every curse word she knew.

The windshield fogged.

When she finished, she checked her face in the passenger mirror and arranged her bangs. Then she got out and went back inside.

Jimmy followed a minute later.

———o———

ABOUT THE AUTHOR

C.j. Roark

When she's able to tune out the voices in her head, C.J. enjoys spending time with her husband, daughter, and four cats. While she dreams of someday escaping to an English country cottage, she would prefer to do so with her family rather than any one of her characters (although Georgie would make an awesome BFF.)

www.ingramcontent.com/pod-product-compliance
Lightning Source LLC
Chambersburg PA
CBHW051144130726
47988CB00005B/1980